Vintage

Venus

And Other Stories

Edited by

JULIA T. LYE

DeeBee

Vintage Venus

For information contact David Allan Hamilton:

davidallanhamilton00@gmail.com

www.deebeebooks.com

ISBN: 9781896794334

First Edition: January 2020

10 9 8 7 6 5 4 3 2 1

CONTENTS

U-27

By Steph Fantin

IT STARTED WITH A BLUEBERRY SCONE.

Richard Brix had been going to the same cafe for breakfast for the last eight years. In those eight years he had never managed to get there early enough to snag one of their famous blueberry scones. Today he happened to arrive a few minutes before he normally did, and sitting in the little wicker basket was a single blueberry scone. It was a miracle. It was just as good as he imagined.

When he arrived at the office he dropped his bag on his desk and looked around in confusion. His coworker Brent, who sat at the desk across from him, wasn't there to call out, "Good morning Dick!" like he did every single day with his customary shit-eating grin. He had been called that for years by the bullies at the orphanage and it was never funny.

"Did you hear what happened?" Marcia, the office busybody, suddenly appeared at his cubicle.

Richard shook his head, knowing if he kept his eyes fixed on his computer and didn't respond with words she would lose interest and go away.

"Brent was sharing client information. They walked him out this morning!"

His boss called him into his office and told him he would be taking over Brent's clients in a more senior position at the company. Juliette, the cute admin assistant, invited him to drinks with the rest of the team that Friday night to celebrate. And on his way home, an enthusiastic sign spinner outside a pizza shop knocked into him and felt so bad he sent Richard home with a free pizza.

Overall it had been a strange day. He got to have a blueberry scone, his bully was fired, he got a promotion and a free pizza, so why didn't he feel happy about any of it?

Richard dropped the pizza box on the counter, loosening his tie as he made his way to the bathroom. He looked at himself in the mirror and frowned. His brown hair had a few threads of grey, and the bags around his eyes and mouth made him look older than thirty eight. He attempted an awkward smile but it looked more like a grimace.

His heart pounded in his chest. He ran the cold water and splashed his face then took a deep breath. A wave of nausea made his stomach roll and he gripped the edge of the sink.

"Get it together, Rich, " he muttered.

This was just a panic attack and it would pass if he got it under control. His ears started to ring, quietly at first, but when the nausea hit him again it grew louder. Richard wondered if he was dying.

Blood dripped from his nose, bright red against the white porcelain sink. The taste of it filled his mouth and he retched, then vomited into the sink. It spattered his arms and the front of his suit jacket but he barely noticed. Richard sunk to his knees and vomited again on the linoleum floor. The ringing in his ears was deafening, it was going to drive him crazy. Richard curled up on the floor, sweating and shaking until the ringing in his ears finally quieted and was replaced with the pounding of his heart.

Cool tile beneath his cheek startled him awake. He pushed himself up and squinted at his new digital watch, but the screen was blank and dead. How long had he been lying there? His body was stiff and sore, his head still ached, and his mouth tasted like blood and vomit and cotton balls. He rubbed the sleep from his eyes, focusing on the row of shiny metal stalls in front of him.

Richard jumped to his feet, and had to brace himself on the sink when his head spun. He didn't know where he was and he definitely had never been here before. A sign scrolling along the bottom of the mirror read ASK YOUR DOCTOR IF BIOPLAST™ IMPLANTS ARE RIGHT FOR YOU. His fingers touched smooth glass and he wondered how they made it look like it was a part of the mirror. He looked past the writing to see his vomit spattered jacket and cringed, then pulled the jacket off and stuffed it into the garbage can.

When he stepped out the door he discovered he was at a bar. It looked like a normal bar at first glance, but as his eyes passed over the room again he realized it was unlike anything he had ever seen. The walls had moving pictures that changed every few seconds, there were glowing lights in colours he hadn't thought possible, and even the people looked strange. A woman with a shaved head and spikes through her lip sat in a booth with a man wearing an indecent shirt. Three old men in robes looked up at him when he opened the door but quickly went back to arguing loudly.

"Bathrooms are for customers only!" the barkeep called out.

"I'll take a gin and tonic." Richard patted his back pocket for his wallet, relieved to find it still with him, and walked up to the bar.

"What?"

"A gin and tonic?" Richard repeated, furrowing his brow.

"Don't have that here."

"Fine just give me anything." Richard sighed.

"Fifteen credits, " he said and set down a glass of bright red liquid in front of him.

"Credits?" He tried to hand the barkeep a twenty and the barkeep looked at him strangely.

"I don't want some bit of paper." The barkeep picked up a remote and pointed it at him.

"B-but I don't have anything else!" The barkeep rolled his eyes and pressed a button, shining a red light into Richard's eyes and causing him to flinch. "Hey man watch it!"

"Richard Brix. Fifteen credits, " said a robotic female voice. Richard whipped his head around, looking for whoever it came from.

"You're good."

The drink was bitter and sugary sweet. The alcohol burned in his chest and settled his shaking hands. The initial panic had faded and he could finally think. He had gotten violently sick, passed out on his bathroom floor and woke up at a bar he had never seen before. A bar that didn't even accept the dollar! Was he dead? Was this the afterlife?

When he asked the barkeep, the man laughed at him and shook his head as he walked away.

Richard didn't know how he had gotten here, wherever here was, and he didn't care anymore. He just wanted to go home to the new episode of Star Trek and his pizza. He downed his drink and stumbled back to the bathroom. He curled up on the floor and closed his eyes, hoping that when he opened them again he would be home.

The floor was cold and disgusting and after a few minutes he accepted it wasn't going to work. He staggered into one of the stalls and slumped on the toilet as he tried to think of something to do. There was another moving picture on the back of the stall door featuring an explicit condom advertisement. Nothing made sense and he knew he couldn't go back out there.

The bathroom door creaked open and he heard the sound of heavy footsteps. One of the stall doors was thrown open with a loud bang and Richard jumped at the sudden noise. They continued down the line to the end stall where he was now perched on top of the toilet, frozen in terror. The door to his stall rattled but held.

"Occupied!"

"Open the door, " said a deep, gravelly voice.

Richard sat silent and trembling on the toilet seat, hoping if he was quiet enough they would leave. There was a long pause, then the door shuddered once, then twice, before slamming open so hard it bounced off the wall. Richard shrieked and collapsed to the floor, covering his head with his arms.

A man and a woman stood over him, both built like linebackers and dressed in identical black suits. Their short dark hair was slicked back and large dark sunglasses hid most of their face.

"Get up."

"What do you want?" Richard picked himself up off the floor for the third time that day.

"Richard Brix."

It wasn't a question but Richard shook his head reflexively. "Sorry I think you have the wrong man."

From the blank look on their faces he could see they weren't convinced.

"Come with us."

"Come where? Who are you?" His eyes darted around the room as he looked for a way out. The man looked over to the woman and nodded. The woman reached into her breast pocket and pulled out a small silver tube and point it right at his face.

"Hey what is that? Is this like one of those Men in Black things?" He raised his hands to protect his face but she had already pressed down on the top. A fine mist shot out and Richard choked on the noxious smell of citrus and parmesan.

"What did you do to me?" he tried to ask, but his tongue felt thick in his mouth and he could barely get the words out. The bar bathroom swam in front of him and he stumbled, pressing his hand on the bathroom stall to steady himself.

"Catch him, " he heard her say before everything went black.

He came to in the back of a van. Thing 1 and Thing 2 wrenched open the doors and grabbed him by the arms, lifting him out.

"Let me go! I can do it myself." Richard scowled in an attempt to look braver than he felt. The man snorted and let go. He tried to take a step and his knees buckled under him. They grabbed him by the arms again before he could topple forward.

It was only a little embarrassing to have them frog-march him through a warehouse, but the flurry of noise and activity quickly distracted him. Men and women were huddled over floating screens, waving their hands and switching the images so fast he couldn't see what they were looking at. The noises of machinery echoed from somewhere he couldn't see. No one seemed to notice, or even care, that these two goons were pushing a kidnapping victim through the room. They entered a small office, one of the only enclosed spaces in the warehouse, and dumped Richard face first onto a stained brown couch that had clearly seen better days.

"Richard, welcome." A smooth British accent drew his attention to the corner of the room. Behind a desk sat a small, dark skinned man with a neat beard and a kind smile. "Can I get you something to drink? Eat?"

The thought of food made him notice that beyond the pain and fatigue, there was a desperate dryness in his mouth and a hollow pang of hunger in his stomach.

"Yes. Both, " he replied. The man nodded to Thing 1 and Thing 2, who let themselves out of the office and shut the door behind them.

"I'm sure you have a lot of questions. My name is Saleem. I'd like to apologize for the way you were brought here but I hope I can explain to you why it was necessary."

"I hope so too." Richard said. They were interrupted by the arrival of a woman who introduced herself as Fawn. She handed Richard a bottle of water and a sandwich.

"I'll explain as best I can while you eat and then you can ask whatever you like."

Richard took a long drink and then unwrapped the sandwich. It was nothing special, ham and mustard, a bit on the dry side, but he tore into it like it was the best thing he had ever tasted.

"It's a bit complicated but essentially, you've crossed over from another universe."

Richard choked. Saleem and Fawn watched him but made no move to help as he hacked and coughed.

"What the fuck?" he wheezed, "is this a joke?"

"Unfortunately for you, it's not. Come now, you must have realized this is not where you came from." Saleem looked at him with a pitying smile.

Richard refused to answer, staring at the floor instead. His sandwich suddenly didn't seem that appealing anymore.

"We call them crossings. There's a rip in the fabric between worlds, and sometimes people fall through." Saleem continued. He flicked his wrist and a screen appeared in the air. It showed the Earth slowly rotating. "This is the Earth of your universe. We refer to it as U-28."

He pinched his fingers and the Earth shrunk, surrounded by the planets and stars of the Milky Way. One more twitch of his fingers and the image flattened to a disk. Richard's eyes widened at the display, he had never seen anything like it. He waved a hand and another disk appeared above the first. Saleem waved a hand and hundreds of similar disks slid into place, forming a long column of light. "This is our approximation of how it works. There are an infinite number of universes layered on top of each other. Crossings allow you to pass to a universe on either side. There was a tear created between our universe and yours, and you happened to be in the wrong place at the wrong time. Welcome to U-27."

Richard abandoned his sandwich. He could feel a headache coming on. There were so many questions- how did this happen? How come nobody knew about this? Was this even real? Instead, he asked the only question that mattered.

"How do I get home?"

Saleem gave that same pitying expression and Richard felt a flicker of annoyance. He had seen that expression many times before. It was on the matron's face when she told him he wouldn't be going home with the nice couple who came to meet him, and the social worker's when she picked him up from the foster home. The annoyance turned into the sick feeling of dread when he realized what was coming.

"Richard, you can't go home."

"That can't be right." He was already shaking his head in denial. "Isn't there another tear I can go back through?"

"It doesn't work like that, " Fawn finally spoke up. "We only know about them after they've happened."

"This is a joke. This isn't happening. I need to leave." Richard tried to stand on shaking legs.

"Sit back down. There is more to tell you and frankly, it's going to get worse." Saleem's voice was cold and bore no room for argument. Richard wanted to rebel, just for the sake of it, but the fight left him and he slumped back down on the couch instead.

"How can it get worse?"

"You're not the only Richard Brix in U-27. It's a paradox the universe can't ignore. It will try to correct itself, and you don't want to find out what happens if it can't."

The room filled with broken, haunted laughter and it took a minute for Richard to realize it was coming from him. Fawn and Saleem traded wary looks and Richard desperately tried to get himself under control.

"Of course." His voice came out in a gasp and a shrill giggle escaped his mouth. "This is insane. This is fucking insane."

The office door opened and a man poked his head in. He stared at Richard, who was still fighting back giggles. "Did he crack? That's stellar. Dido owes me five credits."

"You disappoint me Orrick." Fawn said, her kind face twisting into a scowl.

"Sorry Fawn, " he replied with a mocking smile, clearly not sorry at all. Orrick let himself into the room and sprawled out on the couch beside Richard, running a hand through greasy red hair.

"Look mate, you're no use to us if you're cracked, " he told Richard.

"No use to you?"

Orrick faked an innocent smile, ignoring Saleem, who was giving him an angry pointed look. "Oh, he didn't explain?"

"Explain what?" He was already so tired, he didn't know how much more life shattering information he could take.

"Our universe deviated very early on from yours. Organized religion never really took off, which allowed the development of the sciences to happen much earlier. Here, the first industrial revolution started in 1688. We had electricity before the 1700's." Fawn explained.

"We don't have time for a history lesson right now." Orrick said. Fawn ignored him.

"Developing technology became a competition between nations and governments stopped protecting people in favour of capitalizing on it. There have been so many horrific acts done to humans, animals, the environment, all in the name of science. There are no laws to protect any of us, not when the people in charge are the ones responsible."

"That's why we're here, " Saleem cut in, "we have all been affected by the government's disregard for our lives. We came together as a resistance to undermine their control and mitigate some of the destruction they have caused."

An underground resistance. An exploitative government. The pieces began to click into place and Richard had to remind himself that this was real and it was actually happening to him. Saleem flicked his fingers at the screen again and an image of his own face was projected.

"This is Richard Brix of U-27."

There were subtle differences but the sense of déjà vu was overwhelming. This Richard Brix was sharper, stronger, and the set of his shoulders and chin showed a confidence that Richard himself never had.

"He grew up much like you did. His parents died in a car wreck when he was four. He lived in an orphanage and several different foster homes until he was adopted by the Plaskett family."

Richard remembered living with the Plasketts. They were an older couple who fostered several children in their lifetime. He had lived with them for three years and for a little while he thought he might be happy there, until Mrs. Plaskett had a heart attack. Mr. Plaskett couldn't take care of all the children as well as Mrs. Plaskett, so he had been sent back to the orphanage.

"Richard enlisted in the military when he was eighteen and quickly moved into Special Operations, which he is now the head of. He married Lydia Berkman and they have two children together."

Lydia Berkman. He rolled the name around in his head before the image of a little girl with skinned knees and curly red hair came to mind. They had lived together at the Plasketts. She had been his only friend back then, a friendship was born from their shared pain at being in the foster system. When they were separated, he hadn't been able to contact her and in the following years he had forgotten about her entirely. This Richard had gotten to stay and grow up with a family and a friend. No wonder he looked so good.

"Why are you telling me this?" It came out more bitter than he intended.

Saleem's calm and gentle expression suddenly changed. He was hard, focused. The sharp lines of his face were highlighted by the glowing screen and his black eyes shone with something Richard couldn't identify.

"The resistance is losing ground. Frankly, Richard Brix is too good at his job, and his job is to prevent domestic terrorism. If we had a man on the inside, we would be able to prepare accordingly. We need you."

"What are you getting at?" Richard asked, but by the sinking feeling in his stomach he thought he already knew.

"We want you to kill Richard Brix and assume his life. Report to us and help us undermine the government where we can, " Saleem said.

Richard burst into laughter again.

THE COM LIT UP AS SOON AS HE ARRIVED AT HIS DESK. HE LET OUT A SMALL groan when he saw the name on the display. It was never a good sign when his boss called him this early in the morning.

"Brix! Get up here!" The Colonel snapped as soon as he answered and then hung up on him. Technically he was Lieutenant Colonel Brix, but the Colonel had never been fussy about proprieties. Though Colonel O'Keel was his superior officer they had been friends for many years and had worked together for longer.

Richard Brix from U-27 waved a hand to dispel his holoscreen and got up from his desk.

"In trouble already?" Captain Amanda Hawke grinned up at him from her desk.

"It's going to be one of those days." He nodded and made his way up two floors to the Colonel's office.

The secretary gave him a small, nervous smile as she waved him into the office.

"Sir?" asked Brix, not waiting for permission to take a seat.

The Colonel brought up his holoscreen with a strong jab of his fingers. He lacked finesse in most areas, preferring to operate with blunt efficiency. "We received a flag on your account. Someone used your credentials to pay for a drink at The Black Penny."

He swiped across the screen and a video loaded. Brix watched as a man stumbled out of the bathroom. He paused at the door, and the Colonel zoomed in on his face. Brix felt a cold chill run down his spine when he saw his own face looking back at him. He watched himself have a drink at the bar and then run back to the bathroom. Minutes later, two people came into the bar, their faces blurred. Brix watched the two figures drag a third out of the bar. They had applied the same scrambler to the third, though it was presumably himself they were dragging out.

"That can't be right. I've never been there sir."

"We've checked the footage, it hasn't been manipulated."

"Any luck fixing the distortion field?"

"Unfortunately it's impossible to correct, " the Colonel confirmed.

"I don't know what to make of this, " Brix said. He checked the time stamp on the video. "This can't be me. I was home all night, ask my wife."

"We have." The Colonel looked at him with a steady gaze, and seemed to come to some conclusion. "U-DEV confirmed there was an anomaly at that location minutes before your identity was used."

Brix let out a long breath and sat back in the chair. He knew what that meant. It was him in the video, just a different version of him.

"You're going to have to bring him in."

"Yes sir, " Brix replied absently. His head was elsewhere. He had to tell Lydia. How would he explain this to the kids?

"We need to keep this between us, " the Colonel added, as if he had read his mind.

"Sir, wouldn't it make more sense to share this intel? We need as many eyes on him as we can get."

"And put the credibility of our department at risk? It only invites dissonance if your identity is in question. We can't allow the rebels to use this opportunity to ruin us."

"That's a bullshit answer sir, and you know it."

"Well that's what came down from upstairs, " the Colonel shrugged. "I don't give a shit about office politics but when we're given an order, we follow it and we don't ask why."

Brix didn't like that answer but he knew the conversation was over. He got up from his seat and made for the door.

"Oh and Brix?"

"Yes sir?"

"Bring him in *alive*."

WHEN RICHARD FINALLY CALMED DOWN, SALEEM SHOWED HIM AROUND the warehouse that served as their base. There were fifty-three active members of the resistance. He was introduced to so many people, he stopped trying to keep their names and faces straight.

Richard was still in a daze about the whole thing. How was he supposed to kill a Spec Ops agent? He'd never even held a gun! It would be better to take himself out of the picture. It was the easiest option, considering it was most likely to end in the same result. This way he wouldn't have to murder someone. Or would it be considered suicide? He tried not to smile at the thought. They already thought he was losing his mind.

Richard was introduced to a woman named Sarge. He was so distracted it took him a moment to notice something odd. He looked down in surprise and almost dropped the metal claw in his hand. Her whole arm was metal, right up to the shoulder.

She grinned. "It's alright kid, everyone's a little shocked at first."

Richard didn't much appreciate being called kid but he was hesitant to say so. Sarge had about twenty years on him and could knock him flat with one look from her strange, mismatched eyes. One eye was a normal cloudy blue and the other steely silver. The silver eye moved independently, making him jump back in surprise, and she cackled with laughter.

"Sarge is ex-military, " Fawn said, "she's the best sniper in the world."

"Yeah well having a robotic arm and eye helps."

"Sarge here is going to train you in combat and shooting, " Saleem told him.

"Wait a second. I haven't agreed to anything yet, " Richard said.

"Do you really think there's a choice?" Orrick asked in outrage.

"I'm not a murderer!" Richard shouted back. "I don't want to kill anyone and honestly, I don't even think I can. He's a fucking Spec Ops agent. How am I supposed to beat that?"

Orrick sneered. "So what, you'd rather die?"

"Obviously not. I'd *rather* go home." Richard crossed his arms, doubling down on his position.

"Richard we've told you this. There is no going home." Saleem frowned.

"How do you know? Maybe I should turn myself in. If the government is creating these tears maybe they can figure out how to send me back, " Richard replied stubbornly.

"Come with me." Saleem turned and walked away, not waiting to see if they would follow.

They came upon a workstation littered with tools and machinery where a man sat in front of several screens, typing furiously and muttering to himself.

"Dr. Wayland." The man held up one finger at Saleem and continued to type for another minute, leaving the group standing awkwardly while he finished. With a nod and a satisfied smile, he finally swivelled in his chair to face them.

"What can I do for you?" Dr. Wayland was a small balding man with dark circles around his eyes like he hadn't gotten much sleep.

"This is Richard. He crossed from U-28, " Saleem said.

"Of course! Pleasure to meet you." The man looked him up and down with a critical eye, and Richard shifted uncomfortably. It was like he was being analyzed under a microscope."Do you think I could take a few blood and tissue samples? Nothing too invasive. I am just fascinated by the differences in our universes and would love to study it at a cellular level."

Richard looked to Saleem who gave a small shrug."Alright. I guess."

"Dr. Wayland was the first to discover the structure of the alternate universes. He helped develop U-DEV, the branch responsible for the crossings, " Saleem explained.

"I prefer to call them parallel universes, " Dr. Wayland said, tugging on Richard's arm to put him in his seat. He rolled up the sleeve of Richard's dirty, white button-up."the universes are arranged parallel to each other, and based on the consistency of the-"

"We don't need a lesson Doc, " Orrick cut in.

"There must be a way to get back, " Richard said. The needle pinched as it went into his arm and Dr. Wayland quickly drew a few vials of blood.

"I'm afraid not. The experiments run by U-DEV do open crossings but that was never the intention. There is no way to be sure which way the crossing will work. It drew you in from U-28 and spat you out here but it was just as likely to take someone from here and put them into U-26. Or take someone from U-26 and bring them here." Dr. Wayland cocked his head, looking thoughtful."Then there is the possibility of time displacement. There are just too many variables."

Richard felt lightheaded. He wasn't sure if it was from having his blood taken or the realization he was never going home. He followed Dr. Wayland's instructions numbly, opening his mouth to allow him to swab his cheek, barely flinching as he pulled a few strands of hair.

"Relax kid." Sarge squeezed his shoulder with her metal claw."You can't go home but you can make a good life here. Think of it as a second chance."

"I'm going to die here."

"Well all you can do is try right?" Fawn smiled encouragingly."And we'll be here to help you."

In the next few days Richard began his lessons and the results were not promising.

Saleem gave him a rundown of the government and political situation. Orrick gave him lessons on basic technology. He met Dido, a teenage boy who followed Orrick around like a shadow, who taught him about all the strange slang words he would need to know, as well as popular culture from the past and present. Fawn instructed him on the finer points of Brix's life, including eerily specific details like favourite meals, first kiss, and the layout of his house. It was a lot to take in at once and he found himself slipping up over and over.

But his biggest failure was with Sarge. Sarge started by teaching him basic hand-to-hand and gun safety. Richard consistently failed, getting hit in the face and missing his punches repeatedly. He also could never seem to remember how to assemble a pistol except when Sarge was doing it step by step beside him. Overall, he was exhausted, sore, and just plain defeated. He wondered if Brix ever felt like this or if everything just came easier to his alternate self.

Sarge let him fire a gun on the fifth day. As expected, he did miserably, dropping the rifle when it kicked back into his shoulder for the first time and not once hitting the target. Sarge was always a good sport, offering encouraging words and repositioning his grip every time.

"This is a waste of time." Richard heard Orrick's voice from behind him as he tried to line up his shot."He's never going to get better. We should just cut our losses and let him go."

"Shut up Orrick, " Fawn snapped.

"You were pretty fucking useless when you first joined us too, " Sarge reminded him.

"At least I could hold a gun without dropping it, " Orrick said in defense."at least I can throw a punch without crying about it!"

Richard tried to ignore the voices behind him. He took a deep breath and pulled the trigger. He flinched at the sound of the gun firing and the bullet went wide, again. Orrick was right, he was useless. He was never going to get it and he was running out of time. Last night he had gotten a wicked headache and started bleeding from the nose and ears. Saleem had explained this was an effect of the paradox, that the universe was trying to kill him.

"We're wasting our time and resources, " Orrick continued."they already know he's here and it's only a matter of time before they find him."

"What?" Richard spun around to face them, forgetting he was still holding the rifle.

Sarge growled at him and wrenched the gun out of his hands. Everyone glared at Orrick, who had his hands up in front of him.

"Brix knows you're here. He's looking for you, " Fawn said."we didn't want to tell you and stress you out even further."

"I'm dead, " Richard laughed, shaking his head."I'm fucking dead. There's no point to this. I should just do you a favour and do the job for him."

There was a chorus of outrage from everyone except Orrick.

"Stop this immediately." Saleem appeared at his side."Orrick, take Dido and go on a supply run."

Orrick gave him a mocking salute and slunk off to find Dido. Saleem turned to Richard, his mouth set in a firm line. Richard shrunk in on himself, his shoulders creeping up to his ears as he wavered under Saleem's hard look. He felt like he was back in the orphanage, being scolded by the matron.

"Stand up straight, " Saleem barked and Richard jumped to comply. "Brix doesn't let himself be cowed by a twenty year old boy. He doesn't give up just because the work seems hard."

"But I'm not him!" Richard said desperately. "I don't know how to do this!"

"You'll learn. But if you don't start acting like him then you're never going to be him." Saleem turned on his heel and strode off. Sarge gave him a comforting pat on the shoulder with her real hand.

"Come on kid, let's try something else."

BRIX HAD BEEN LOOKING FOR LEADS FOR DAYS NOW AND WAS STILL COMING up short.

The rebels had the sympathy of the general public but there were plenty of ways to get information. It was always handy for Spec Ops to have a few birds, those who were open to selling what they knew to anyone who would pay. Pollux was one example, a known criminal who fenced stolen tech. Brix kept tabs on the man and once in a while used him to find out what the rebels were looking for.

Pollux said didn't have anything to tell him but Brix knew how to read people and he knew when they were lying. He never liked wasting a resource, especially one as good as Pollux, but his bosses were breathing down his neck for results and the faster he caught the man the safer his family would be. So when Pollux denied knowing anything, Brix broke both his legs. When he continued to deny him, he moved to his fingers. He got through four of the fingers on his left hand when Pollux finally caved. In between sobs, he told Brix that the rebels were scheduled to pick something up from him this evening at the trainyard.

Brix thanked him by putting a bullet through his head.

He had been waiting at the trainyard for hours. It was dark except for the ambient light from the city. Lydia had called him a few times when he failed to return home at his usual time. All he could do was send her a quick message telling her he wasn't sure when he would be home and not to wait up. He had been distant from her the last few days. He never liked keeping things from her and something as important as this was killing him. But the Colonel refused to allow him to tell his wife, even if it put her at risk.

A car pulled into the trainyard, it's lights off. Brix watched from his vantage point as two men got out and breathed a sigh of relief. Two men he could handle by himself. He peered through the scope of his rifle, slowing his breaths as he waited for them to move into a better position. They waited there completely exposed like idiots. Brix fired two quick shots hitting both targets easily.

The men lay sprawled on the ground. They were both younger than he expected, still just boys. He pushed the thought from his mind. There was no time to be sentimental when he had a job to do. Their vitals confirmed they were still alive and the tranquilizer darts he had shot them with were doing their job. It only took him a few minutes to tie them up and load them into his van.

Brix had them gagged and tied to a chair before they awoke. The younger of the two began to struggle, rubbing his wrists raw against the restraints as he tried to get free. The older of the two grunted to try and get his attention. Brix watched the exchange with consideration. The younger one would be the easiest to crack but who knew what the older of the two would say when he applied a bit of pressure.

"I would stop struggling if I were you, " Brix said casually from behind them. The boys tried to turn their heads to see him but the restraints wouldn't let them get that far. "You're only going to hurt yourself and I'll be doing enough of that for you."

"I want you to think very carefully about my next words. I'm looking for Richard Brix. I know your little group of rebels have him. Tell me where he is and I'll let you live." They both went still at his words and Brix smiled. It was easy manipulating people's fears. He knew how to reach people, how to use the right words to get the reaction he wanted. It was a skill he had learned early in life as he moved around from foster home to foster home, before the Plasketts.

He pulled off their gags and moved to stand in front of the boys.

"What are your names?"

"Don't say a word, " the older boy said sharply.

Brix sighed and swiftly slapped the young boy across the face. He cried out in pain and the older boy gave an angry shout, spewing threats as he struggled against his bonds.

"Dido, " the young boy said through his tears, "My name is Dido. He's Orrick."

"Stop talking!" Orrick shouted.

"Thank you, Dido." Brix smiled. "Will you tell me where I can find Richard Brix?"

Dido opened his mouth again but snapped it shut at a glare from Orrick.

"He's standing right in front of me." Orrick spat.

Brix normally would have been impressed by the kid's guts but today he just didn't have time for it. He drew his fist back and punched Orrick in the face twice in quick succession. Blood ran from his nose into his mouth, dripping down his chin to stain his shirt.

Dido was sobbing now. Brix bent down so he could look Dido in the eyes.

"Tell me what I want to know and I'll stop."

"Promise?" Dido asked.

Brix smiled. "I promise."

"Dido, don't you dare tell him anything!" Orrick said. Dido looked over at him and bit his lip. Brix stood up and delivered a swift punch to Orrick's gut, effectively shutting him up. He punched him a few more times, enough to do some damage, but more so to provoke cries of pain.

"I'm sorry Orrick, I can't. I can't let him hurt you, " Dido sobbed.

Brix rolled his eyes at the theatrics. "I'm running out of patience."

"We have Richard. He's at our base."

Dido was more than forthcoming when it came to the rest of his questions, like who was in charge, what weapons they had, and how many people were at the base.

"And where is this base?" Brix asked. Dido relayed a set of coordinates, barely heard over the sounds of Orrick's angry shouts.

"Thanks son." Brix smiled at the boy who sagged in relief. Brix drew his pistol and shot Dido in the head. Orrick stared at him in shock and horror, before howling with rage and struggling against his bonds.

"You promised!"

"I promised I wouldn't hurt you, " agreed Brix, levelling the pistol at his head. "You'll be dead before you feel a thing."

"Bastard!"

"Anything you want to add before you join him?"

Orrick grinned, blood staining his gums and teeth red. He looked like a wild animal. "He's going to kill you. He's going to fucking-"

The shot went off and Orrick's words died with him.

RICHARD FOUND HIMSELF LOITERING AROUND DR. WAYLAND'S workstation, listening to the man describe his current project. It had something to do with time travel or manipulating time, Richard wasn't exactly sure. He didn't really understand the man's jargon and when he really got going on a tangent, he was almost incomprehensible. In a rare break in the doctor's words, Richard finally had the opportunity to ask what was on his mind.

"Doctor, what exactly was your department doing that caused the crossings?"

Dr. Wayland looked up at him from the small device he was tinkering with and then surprised him by setting down his tools. It was rare to have the doctor's undivided attention.

"We were trying to study the parallel universes by creating a window by which we could view them. In our hubris we failed to realize that what we were doing would have a bigger impact on the fabric between universes than we expected. The machine created instabilities that rippled through space and time and created crossings we had no control over."

"There's a machine? Do they still have it?" Richard asked.

"I would assume so." Dr. Wayland shrugged, absently touching the chain at his neck. "Though they would never be able to operate it. I created a safeguard so the machine could not be operated without the only key.

Besides-"

An explosion rocked the building.

The lights flickered but stayed on. People were screaming over the sound of rapid gunfire and Richard stood in shock as it unfolded around him. Dr. Wayland immediately turned to his screens and started typing quickly. He pulled out several small boxes from the computer and handed one to Richard.

"Keep that safe. It's a backup of all my research. The more copies I have the better." Richard only nodded and stuffed the box in the pocket of his borrowed combat pants. The shots sounded closer to them and Richard took off running.

"Time to go! Not that way." Sarge intercepted him, armed to the teeth. Two rifles were slung over her back and another in her hand. She turned him around and pushed him back the direction he had come from.

"What happened?"

"It's Brix. He's come for you."

Richard followed Sarge through the chaos. Sarge dropped into one of the mechanics bays. He heard her curse loudly and scrambled after her. Dr. Wayland was sprawled on the floor. He only knew it was him because of the lab coat and silver chain glinting from around his bloody neck. He must have been hiding in there and poked his head above the edge of the bay only to have it blown off.

Richard fought back the urge to be sick and lost, spewing vomit across the floor. Sarge didn't give him a second look, she was focused on fighting back the onslaught of agents. Richard crouched down with his back pressed against the wall. He couldn't take his eyes off the body. He was going to ask Dr. Wayland to help him get home. He had the only key. Richard was suddenly reminded of how the doctor touched the chain at his neck. The chain that had a silver pendant on it. Before he could think too much about it, Richard pulled the chain from the doctor's neck.

"Richard Brix!" He heard his name called. It felt like he was hearing his own voice on tape. Brix had found him. The staccato pops of gunfire were closer now, the sound was almost deafening.

"Richard, are you still with me? You're going to have to make a run for it!" Sarge shouted. Two of her rifles lay empty on the ground. He wiped his bloody hands on his pants and shoved the chain into his pocket along with the box. He poked his head above the lip of the bay and quickly ducked back down. There were too many of them. They would never fight them back.

Sarge dropped the last rifle, out of extra rounds, and hunched down for cover as she drew a pistol. She was shouting something at him but he couldn't hear anything but the pounding of his heart. Sarge popped back up to fire and was struck back by a shot that went right through her shoulder. She dropped with a small cry of pain, blood running down her arm.

"Drop the weapon!" A voice shouted from above them. A female agent in black body armour pointed an assault rifle at Sarge. Sarge gritted her teeth and then dropped the gun, raising her hands in surrender. Richard copied her movements, kneeling on the ground and putting their hands behind their heads.

"Take him." Richard heard his voice before he saw him.

He stared up at Richard Brix of U-27 and Richard stared back at him. It was like looking into a funhouse mirror. They stared silently at each other as the woman jumped into the bay and pulled Richard's hands behind his back, cuffing them. Brix jumped into the bay after her, gun still trained on Sarge.

"Sergeant Ohura. It's a shame we had to meet like this, " Brix said. They had the same voice, but Brix had such a smooth confidence that it was almost unrecognizable.

Sarge said nothing and stared past him. The female agent wrenched Richard to his feet and trained her pistol on Sarge. Brix moved forward to cuff her, but Sarge's metal arm moved faster than humanly possible and swung at his knee. Brix jerked back just in time to avoid having his kneecap shattered. The female agent was shouting now, warning that she would shoot, but Brix raised a hand.

"Let me take care of this, Captain."

Brix was an even match for Sarge's skill and speed, even with her metal arm and pinpoint accuracy. Sarge clawed him across the chest, the blow glancing off his body armour. Brix feinted to one side and then hit her with an uppercut that was no more than a blur. They danced around each other and Richard realized with horror that Brix was toying with her. As he was being dragged away he watched over one shoulder as Brix brought Sarge to her knees. He broke Sarge's other arm and produced a blade from nowhere. He looked up and met Richard's eyes, his face expressionless as he yanked her head back by the hair and cut her throat.

Richard went limp and allowed himself to be dragged out of the warehouse without a fight. There was nowhere else to go at this point. No other moves he could make. The Captain pushed him out the doors and he felt fresh air for the first time since he had come to this universe. The air smelled wrong, like smoke and ash. He wondered if it was always like this or if it was a product of the carnage inside the warehouse.

The Captain dragged him past several officers that were loading prisoners into vehicles. Richard was relieved that some of them managed to escape with their lives. He thought he saw Fawn as she was pushed into the back of a van but he couldn't be sure. There was no sign of Saleem. He wondered if he was dead.

"We've got room for one more in here, " an officer told the Captain as they passed. She shook her head.

"This one goes separately. Boss' orders." She said. The officer shrugged and let her pass. He was forced into the passenger seat of an SUV and she shut the door on him then climbed into the driver's side, starting the car and driving off.

"Where are you taking me?" Richard asked. She didn't answer.

Richard looked out the window as they drove past empty fields of yellow and brown. It was hard to tell the time of day; the sky was smoky grey and blocked out the sun.

"My name is Captain Amanda Hawke. Five years ago, I was brought here from U-26."

That was not what Richard had been expecting at all.

"I killed the Amanda Hawke from this universe and took her place. I helped the resistance as much as I could in the first few years until I learned better." Amanda kept her eyes on the road, her hands gripping the wheel so tightly, he could see her knuckles turning white.

"There's something you need to know. Saleem is a liar. They all are. Or were, " she laughed bitterly.

"What do you mean?" he asked in a quiet voice.

"The crossings are not random and they're not the by-product of government experiments. Well, not anymore, " Amanda said. "Dr. Wayland discovered how to create them but the project was shut down when he proved to be too unstable. He left the government and went to work for the resistance, who allowed him to develop the project until they could get more control over the crossings."

Richard stared at his hands, clenched tightly into fists in his lap.

"They selected us. They brought us here on purpose, feeding us some bullshit story about causing a paradox so we would kill our alternate selves and be their puppets. They're using us."

"How did you find out?"

"I met a scientist who worked in U-DEV with Dr. Wayland. She told me she was still finding signatures all over the place, but they weren't random, they were strategic." There was something sad about the smile on her face and Richard knew this story didn't have a happy ending.

"What happened to her?"

"I went to Saleem and told him I knew what he was doing. I told him I would blow the whole thing if he wasn't straight with me. He told me the truth and said if I didn't keep my mouth shut then he would bring over another Amanda Hawke and replace me. She went missing that night."

Richard was silent for a moment."Do you want to go home?"

"Not anymore." She shook her head."It's been too long and I have a life here now. And if I go back, everything I did would have been for nothing."

"Is he a good man? This world's Richard Brix?"

"He's complicated. He takes his job seriously and will do whatever his superiors tell him, no questions asked. He's done a lot of horrible things in the field doing his job but none of it illegal. He's nice, and friendly, and treats the team well. I know he loves his wife and kids to death. So I don't really know. Does that answer your question?"

He turned his head to look out the window. "I'm not sure."

They drove out of the country and into a suburb where they passed rows of identical houses over and over. Amanda finally pulled the car over and parked on the side of the road and then turned the car off.

"Where are we?" he asked.

"The only place I could think of where you wouldn't be recognized, " Amanda replied. Richard frowned as he looked at the house and then something in his memory clicked.

"You brought me to his house?" Richard flattened himself against the seat and pulled up the collar of his jacket to hide his face.

"He's coming for you whether you like it or not, and when he finds you, he's going to bring you into a research lab where they will poke and prod, and run tests on you until they don't need you anymore, " Amanda replied, "so you need to make a decision on what you're going to do next."

"Isn't he going to know you helped me escape?"

"I'll figure something out."

There wasn't anything left to say. He got out of the car and Amanda drove off, leaving him standing at the end of the driveway looking a little lost. He stared at the house with its perfect, artificial lawn. His house.

Richard squared his shoulders, tilted his jaw and tried to emulate Brix's confidence the way Saleem had told him to. It was like walking into a dream, he thought, taking in the swing and the toys discarded on the porch. The door recognized his face and unlocked, and Richard let himself into the house. He was hit by the smells of home-cooked meals and family and firewood that left him feeling warm.

"I didn't think you were going to be home so early."

Richard had seen pictures of Lydia but they didn't do her justice. Lydia wrapped her arms around him and he sunk into her embrace. He didn't think he had ever been held like this.

"I have to pick something up but then I have to go out again, " he replied, pressing his face to her hair and smelling the unplaceable scent of her shampoo.

"Are you going to be home for dinner? The girls would love to see you when they get home."

"No I'm sorry. I have to get going." Richard really was sorry. He couldn't imagine getting to come home to someone so excited to see him. It made him wonder why he was even trying to go home at all. What did he have there?

"That's alright, they understand." She pressed a kiss to his mouth and Richard cupped the back of her head, kissing her back long and hard. Lydia pulled away with a smile and a wicked grin. "Are you sure you don't have time?"

Richard kissed her again. He should feel guilty for kissing another man's wife but instead, it just felt right. "I can't."

"Well you better be home for breakfast, " she called over her shoulder as she walked down the hall, "I'm making pancakes."

"I can't wait."

Richard went to the office and closed the door. He sat at the desk and pulled up the holoscreen. The box Dr. Wayland had given him rested heavy on his leg, and he pulled it out along with the chain. With no other ideas, he plugged the hard drive in and looked through the files, hoping something would stick out to him. Clicking on a folder labelled Project Bifrost gave him exactly what he was looking for. He scrolled through the data and suddenly felt so much lighter. He finally had a plan. Richard raced out of the office, a wild look in his eyes.

"Honey I'm going to need to borrow your car."

WHEN BRIX GOT HOME, TIRED AND FRUSTRATED AFTER LOSING HIS MARK, he noticed his wife's car wasn't in the driveway. It was odd because he could see her moving around through the kitchen window. His instincts were telling him something was wrong and he rushed into the house.

"I didn't think you would be back so soon, " she said as she stirred something on the stove. Brix slipped an arm around her waist and kissed her cheek.

"What do you mean?"

"You said you weren't going to be home for dinner."

Brix froze. He hadn't talked to Lydia at all today. Richard must have been here. In his house. With his wife.

"I think I left a file when I was here earlier, " Brix lied smoothly as he tried to calm his rattled nerves. "Do you remember what I was doing?"

"I'm not sure but I know you were in your office for a while. Where's my car?" she asked, raising her eyebrows.

"I'll get it back to you don't worry, " Brix said, kissing her on the cheek.

As soon as he left the kitchen, Brix sprinted to his office. The computer wouldn't be able to reproduce everything Richard did on his computer but he would be able to see whatever was on his screen. Richard had connected an external hard drive. He clicked through files with data Brix didn't understand, and it seemed that Richard didn't either at the speed he moved through them. Finally he landed on schematics for a machine of some sort. Richard looked at this page for a long time before opening the browser and searching for an address. Brix copied the address to his holopad and turned off the screen.

It would be stupid for him to go alone, he knew that. But he didn't have time to go back to the office and make a proper plan of attack. He didn't know what Richard was doing at the warehouse or how long he would be there. It was now or never. Besides, if this was official, Brix would be obligated to bring him in alive, and after the bastard made contact with his family, he wasn't feeling that generous anymore.

Under the desk was a small safe set into the floor. Brix unlocked it and pulled out a pistol and ammunition. He loaded the gun and holstered it, checking the safety twice before leaving his office.

"Are you going to tell me where you're going?" Lydia asked, surprising him just outside the office door.

"Not this time, " he replied. She kissed him hard and long, and he allowed himself one moment to enjoy it. Brix let her go and left the house. He didn't let himself look back.

The address led to nothing more than a dilapidated barn in the middle of a field. His wife's car was parked outside, the door left wide open. He approached carefully and could hear the sounds of running machinery inside.

Brix pulled out his gun and clicked the safety off then slipped through the barn doors. The barn was poorly lit with a few flickering bulbs hanging bare from wires along the walls. He followed the sounds of machinery and soft cursing, slipping around machines and sticking to the shadows. Brix poked his head out and saw a huge platform, several holoscreens, and Richard fiddling with a control panel set into the desk.

Brix stepped out of cover and raised his gun.

"Stop what you're doing and raise your hands."

Richard spun around and saw Brix, and then raised his hands and took a small step back. His eyes were wide and scared, an expression Brix had never seen on his own face." Don't shoot me. I'm just trying to figure this out so I can go home."

"Bullshit." Brix looked at this man, a poor facsimile of himself." Why were you at my house?"

"It was the only place I could go."

"What's all this?"

"It's a machine that will take me home. Dr. Wayland invented it when he worked at U-DEV. He used it to bring me here, " Richard said, "he gave me his research before he died. I think I can send myself home."

Sending Richard home would solve all of this. He didn't want to have to kill him, not really, and it was probably better than having a copy of him locked up somewhere to be used against him. Brix climbed the steps to the platform and kept his gun fixed on Richard.

"Do you have a Lydia in your world?" The question slipped out, surprising them both.

Richard nodded slowly. "I did... once."

Brix pressed his lips together and tried to think. Letting him go would mean he failed his mission. He would have to go back to the Colonel and admit he let him go or lie. Neither option sounded that appealing. But as he looked at Richard, who was staring back at him with a familiar determined expression, he knew he would have to go against his orders. Brix lowered the gun but didn't holster it.

"Figure this out now. I want you gone."

Richard sagged in relief. "Thank you."

Brix watched him turn back to the keypad and fiddle with the dials, checking the holoscreen every few seconds as he worked. Finally he took a chain from around his neck, flipped the cover off of a button and inserted a metal tag into the keyhole concealed beneath. He turned the key and pressed down. The machine creaked and groaned as it started up, echoing in the barn. Brix finally looked back at Richard and found a satisfied smile on his face.

"What did you do?"

"I'm sorry Brix." Richard turned to look at him, still smiling.

Dread pooled in his stomach and his head started to pound. He raised his gun again and pointed it at Richard, repeating the question.

"I wouldn't shoot if I were you. And I am you." He chuckled at his own joke. "I don't know what would happen with all this latent energy in the air."

The ache turned into a blinding pain that hit him behind the eyes and Brix's stomach rolled. His ears started to ring, the noise was sharp and loud. He dropped his gun to the floor and clapped his hands over his ears, fighting back the nausea.

"What's happening to me?"

"I figured out how to use the machine but I'm not the one who will be going back. I think I'd like to stay here, " Richard said, "you have it all, Brix, and I think it's time for me to have a win."

"Not a chance, " Brix said through gritted teeth. He ducked down and reached for the gun but suddenly Richard was there. They grappled for it. Brix was stronger but the pain and nausea made his grip weak. Richard tried to wrench the gun out of his hands when it went off with a bang.

The shot blew past Richard and hit the terminal, sending up a shower of sparks. The machines groaned as they slowed. Suddenly, the terminal burst into flames. The machine sparked and there was a crackling sound in the air, like lightning, and in the thunderous boom that followed, it caught fire.

Richard cried out in anger and yanked the gun out of his hands with a sharp tug. Brix wiped blood from his nose and lunged at Richard in one last attempt to get the gun from him. They were grunting and sweating as the fire spread quickly behind them. This had to end now, before the fire got too out of control, before this ringing in his ears drove him crazy, before Richard could kill him. The gun went off again and this time a body hit the floor.

The remains of the barn burned brightly in the dark night.

Richard Brix stumbled away from the barn. Lydia's car caught fire, exploding in a shower of glass and steel. His hands shook, he shouldn't be driving but he had to get away. He had to go home. He knew he couldn't go home looking like this, covered in soot and blood, with a crazed look in his eyes. He cleaned himself up in a public bathroom, changing into the spare uniform he kept in the trunk, and then jumped back in the car and drove home.

His hands had stopped shaking by the time he pulled into the driveway. He let himself into the house, following the sounds of his family to the kitchen. His girls sat at the kitchen table and Lydia stood at the stove, pouring pancake batter into the pan.

"Hey honey." She smiled at him over her shoulder. "You hungry?"

"Sure." He slipped his arms around his wife and rested his chin on her shoulder.

"Chocolate chip?"

"How about blueberry?"

Lot 458

By A. R. Finley

LEXXIN DOME WAS THE ONLY HOME THAT XLV HAD EVER KNOWN. HE couldn't believe that today was the day he'd be leaving forever. The smooth glass walls displayed a pitch-black backdrop, beckoning him to play one last game of Black Hole Skyjacker, but he couldn't spare the time. His bag was packed, essentials only, as instructed. He had just enough time to finish one last lesson.

"Room. Please instruct me."

The walls shimmered away into a seemingly infinite expanse. A soft golden glow surrounded XLV in every direction. He stretched out his arms to either side and gently fell backwards into an invisible cloud, suspending him in mid-air. Room's tranquil voice began to whisper the day's lesson. As he closed his eyes, her voice washed over him and lulled him into a meditative trance.

His mind floated around making connections from Nascency to 16Con. Although he had never faced his truth, his subconscious knew. It knew all the details. He and his siblings were created in Nascency, a biolab where engineers synthesized embryos, genetically altering them to specific criteria, producing their ultimate test subjects. XLV was a synthetic human guinea pig. His fate was sealed and 16Con was the day he would fulfill that destiny.

His words were long and slurred as he asked, "Room?"

"Yes, XLV?"

"What actually happens on 16Con? You have yet to tell me that."

"I am not authorized to give you that information, XLV."

"But… I want to know. I need to know. Please tell me!"

Room did not respond.

"Today's the day, Room. Please!" He fidgeted, his body fighting the trance, "I'm… I'm scared."

XLV felt a slight jolt as his body was raised back to an upright position. His mind began to clear and with it the day's lesson faded away. All traces of their conversation vanished. He slowly opened his eyes. The walls returned to their default sterile steel appearance and the lights flickered back to 6500 Kelvin. Unlike his other lessons, he was left with an odd sinking feeling in the pit of his stomach, but he didn't have time to address it.

"Room. It's time. Thank you for… for everything. I'm going to miss you." He paused for a moment, but Room remained silent. With that, he knew his time at Lexxin Dome was over. "Okay, Room. Please teleport me to Chrysalis."

BLINDING STREAKS OF LIGHT SPARKED IN EVERY DIRECTION. LOUD cracks of electricity sizzled and popped in quick succession. XLV gasped for air as the oxygen was sucked from his lungs. The pungent scent of ozone with subtle hints of copper hung heavy in the air. A dizzying array of images flashed in front of him – Room, meteorites, a white wall, Void, Tromulites, blurs of unknown faces – shuffled and on repeat. His body ripped from one location to another, yet somehow not transporting at all.

One last boom rang out. A long arm appeared out of nowhere, wrapped itself around his waist, and yanked him from his torturous state. He crashed to the ground with a hollow thud and choked as his lungs refilled with air. XLV slowly stood up and scanned the room. A stark white ceiling melted into stark white walls that faded into a stark white floor. All surfaces were splattered with blood and the floor was littered with body parts. A dozen of his siblings had also arrived intact and, like him, stared in disbelief at the scene in front of them.

"Shields up!" boomed a baritone voice.

XLV whipped his head around and craned his neck. Towering above him, a man at least eight feet tall inventoried the room. His weathered face donned a jagged scar etched along his cheekbone. As he took note of the casualties, his silver eyes dulled and the furl in his forehead deepened. Blood dripped from his arm, severed at the wrist, and pooled on the floor around his foot.

"Hello everyone. I am Divinity. I am the head of bioengineering." He looked around the room and locked eyes with each person as he went.

"Welcome to Chrysalis," his voice cracked in betrayal. "I wish it were under better circumstances. Unfortunately, we have been attacked and at a most inopportune time. Somehow the Tromulites knew when you would be teleporting. They intercepted the signals and attempted to obliterate each of you in your molecular state. You are the only ones I could pull out before it was too late. We already have a team investigating the breach."

"I don't understand. We've been allies for centuries. Why would the Tromulites attack us?" asked XLV.

Divinity hung his head low. He took a deep breath before raising his head again, his eyes wrought with pain. "Normally we would let you settle in first, but I guess that is a luxury we can no longer afford. We are indeed at war with the Tromulites and have been for 121 years now. They are trying to lay claim to Keplera for its resources, but as you all know, that is our only source of water, so we cannot let that happen. That's where you come in. You have been bred to be our ultimate soldiers."

As if on cue, a woman with perfectly aligned curls tattooed onto her bald scalp stepped forward. "Hello. I am Aurealia. I will be your doctor. Starting tomorrow you will be receiving injections of $TnSo_7E$. If your genetics were set properly by Nascency, then after a series of injections, you will each develop your nimb, your own unique superpower. And that is how we will win this war!"

Bewildered, no one said a word.

Divinity raised his once severed limb and revealed his newly regenerated hand. "I, too, was born of Nascency. I know this is a lot to take in. When you sleep tonight, your lessons will return to you. Only this time you will remember them all. Now, let's get you to your rooms so you can rest."

XLV ENTERED HIS ROOM AND THE DOOR WHOOSHED SHUT BEHIND him. Inside, the same stark white walls, ceiling, and floor stared back at him. He laid down on his bed and closed his eyes. As the events of the day looped on an endless reel, exhaustion set in, shock faded, and he fell into a fitful sleep.

Echoes of Room's voice bounced around in his mind. Each whisper ignited another lesson, once forgotten, now remembered. Visions danced on the back of his eyelids, accompanying Room's words. As he spiraled through the knowledge base, the stream of information enveloped him in a warm calmness, welcomed after the day's trauma.

A Tromulite, six-foot in stature and nearly as wide, came into view. Impenetrable plate-like scales covered its body from head to toe. It had two sets of arms. The top set adorned chelae and the bottom set housed long sword-like fingers. Venomous barbed antennae sprouted from its head like a deadly crown. Each barb contained a neurotoxin that could place its victim into an indefinite state of suspended animation. They were known for their high intelligence and proved to be the most menacing of all the creatures.

Void came to the forefront next. It was a mysterious phenomenon void of all matter. Not much was known about it. Any attempts at exploration had ended in devastation. Purported rumours swirled amongst the planets that the Tromulites had successfully traversed Void and were using it to imprison their enemies.

As Lesson 2272: Lab Procedures began, a sharp tone sounded and broke his restless slumber. A wave of excitement, steeped in apprehension, swept across his body. Today was the first injection.

THE LAB, FLOODED IN SIMULATED DAYLIGHT, GREETED XLV AND HIS siblings with a false sense of security. Thousands of flexible wands, terminated in microscopic lights, hung from the ceiling and jutted from the walls. The mesh floor clinked underfoot. Twelve chrome chairs, perfectly arranged in a circle, faced each other in anticipation of the events to come.

"Good morning, " offered Aurealia. "Please take your seats so we can get started."

He hesitated for a moment, took a deep breath, and then claimed his spot. As he reclined his chair, individual wands stretched and flexed around him, obliterating any shadows. The cold steel of the chair gnawed at his flesh, but he refused to acknowledge it. With his head cocked at an unnatural angle, he focused on the contents of the tray next to him. A curious hourglass shaped vial stood at attention. It bore its label proudly, Lot 458. Inside, at the bottom, a shimmery black liquid swirled in hypnotic patterns, at the top, a similar white substance danced, and where the two met, a glowing green ring emanated.

"I will now make my way around the room to administer your first injection of synthetic $TnSo_7E$. We've tweaked this batch to be slightly stronger than previous lots. Hopefully this will expedite the development of your nimb." Aurealia lowered her voice, "The shot is going to hurt. I assure you though, the pain will only last for a few minutes. You'll be okay."

Aurealia picked up the vial next to XLV and inserted a syringe, being careful to only draw from the green concoction. She inserted the needle into his arm and depressed the plunger. A searing pain closely trailed the course plotted by the substance as it flowed through his veins. His heart drummed out a rapid-fire S.O.S. Welded shut from the pain, his eyes relentlessly dripped tears to the floor below. Desperate to find something to focus on, he wrenched his eyes open with his fingers. Across the circle, Aurealia pocketed a black-stained syringe before moving on to her next subject.

A blood-curdling shriek erupted and terrorized the room. XLV bolted upright in his recliner, the chair back slapping him in pursuit. To his right, his sister, Circ, flailed violently. Screams turned to a series of stuttered gurgles as blood spilled from her mouth. Her eyes turned backwards in her head. She white-knuckled the edge of her chair as her back arched in an unnatural curve. Her body twitched as though being electrocuted from within. Then, suddenly, silence. Her mangled body slumped awkwardly back into her chair. She was gone.

Aurealia covered Cirq with a sheet. "I'm sorry you all had to witness that." She closed her eyes for a moment, swallowed hard, and patted her lab coat pocket before continuing, "I can see some of you are starting to recover from your injections already. I will check your vitals shortly. Once I have done so, you are free to go."

"BROTHER, UUUUUPP!" SHOUTED L33T AS HE SCOOPED UP THE BACK corner of XLV's chair, raised it high above his head, and tossed it from one arm to the other.

"L33t, put me down."

"Aw, come on! I just got my nimb this week! I want to practice!"

"I know. I get it! Super strength is totally nebacious! But that's what the Pen is for. Plenty of things to pick up and toss around in there. The twins are already in there honing their nimb. I want to watch them. I... I need the distraction."

"Our sisters are at it again? Ha!" L33t lowered him back to the ground. He shuffled his feet and stared at the floor. "Are you worried about tomorrow's injection?"

"Yes." He swallowed hard. "We lost three more of our siblings last week. There are only five of us left now. You and the twins already have your powers. That just leaves Tinsler and me. What if we die? What if we don't get our powers? It's week six. How many more chances do we get?"

L33t grabbed his shoulder in solidarity. He looked him square in the eyes and nodded. "Alright. I hear you... I'll leave you to it then. Enjoy the show." he said before he disappeared behind the Pen doors.

XLV turned his attention back to the observation window and turned on the com. The floor, strewn with charred pieces of a wooden target floating in mini puddles, indicated a battle was imminent. Alpha and Omega had clearly come to a standstill. They stood back-to-back, ready to dual. Every inch of their respective stances screamed fierce warrior. Every inch of their perfectly coiffed hair and immaculate makeup screamed girly-girl princess. He smirked at the contradiction.

"Aaaaaaand, GO!" screamed Alpha.

They each took ten paces forward, turned on their heels, and locked eyes.

Alpha cupped her hands together. As she slowly drew them apart, a ball of orange flames formed.

Omega clenched her fists at her side, knuckle-side up. As the tension mounted in her arms, she raised them up to chest-level.

Alpha squinted her eyes, spun her hands around the molten sphere, and launched it at Omega.

Omega, in turn, twisted her wrists palm-side up, threw open her fingers, and shot long shards of ice from her hands.

Between them, the fire and ice met and created a momentary sparkle of ash dust before vaporizing into oblivion.

XLV sighed. Not even the twin's squabbles could distract him tonight.

DISTRAUGHT WITH GRIEF AND FROZEN IN FEAR, XLV STOOD IN THE doorway of the lab. The death toll hung heavy on his mind. Lot 458 was particularly potent and left no one unscathed. Another injection was a gamble that he didn't want to take, but he knew that was a choice he did not have. He watched as his brother, Tinsler, rushed past him and hopped on one of the empty metal recliners, then forced himself to follow suit. The metal seat, cold and unforgiving, sent a shiver down his spine.

As always, Aurealia located the vein in his arm, inserted the needle, and administered the shot. An immediate lava-like heat circulated throughout his body. Sweat rolled down his face, tears filled his eyes, and the room swam in and out of focus. Through clenched teeth he begged for his nimb to emerge. He begged not to die.

"XLV? XLV, it's over. Come back, " coaxed Aurealia.

As he fought through the brain fog, he struggled to form his words, "I'm h-here."

"How do you feel? Any new sensations?"

After taking stock of himself, he was grateful to be alive, but disheartened that there were no discernable changes. He shook his head.

"Next time. It'll happen next time, " she reassured him as she turned her attention to Tinsler.

XLV faded back into semi-consciousness. Before him, his mind presented him Void. No one had ever seen it and no description existed, yet he knew exactly what it was. A place so dark that even darkness gets lost. He stared into the deep, black nothingness for what seemed like an eternity. Then, suddenly, a face flashed out of the darkness. Aurealia's face. He snapped awake. The remnants of the words *"All black for you, Tinsler"* poked at him.

Concerned for his brother, XLV shouted, "Tinsler?!".

Like a lightning bolt, Tinsler appeared by XLV's side. His nimb had emerged.

THAT EVENING, DIVINITY CALLED AN EMERGENCY MEETING IN THE UTPOD, a small annex just outside Chrysalis. Teleportation was still too risky, so XLV and his siblings snaked their way through underground tunnels to reach their destination. At the end of the passageway, they climbed a set of stairs, pushed through a door, and entered an igloo-shaped room, held erect with silver beams and encased in glass. In the center or the room, a single console stood, seemingly out-of-place. Next to it, Aurealia and Divinity waited for everyone to enter. Outside, a barren landscape was berated by a sandstorm and meteorites streaked the sky.

"Thank you for joining us here. This is the only place that I know is secure. Everything that I am about to tell you, for reasons you will soon understand, needs to remain confidential." Divinity locked eyes with XLV before continuing, "We have determined the source of the security breach that led to the attack by the Tromulites on the day that you arrived. As we had feared, the breach emanated from inside. There is a traitor living amongst us."

Gasps and murmurs erupted around the room. XLV cinched his eyes together and concentrated on the dark narrative that pounded on his skull.

Thud. Thud. A heartbeat raced. Somewhere beyond, interlaced with fear, he heard it, *"Don't react. They don't know it's you. Only one more week and we strike."* His eyes flew open as he recognized the voice. Their plan succeeded and his suspicions were confirmed. "Flank!" he commanded.

L33t, XLV's brother, didn't miss a beat. Like a predator with its prey, he pounced on Aurealia from behind and locked her in a vice-like grip. The sound of her ribs snapping broke through the din. A thin stream of blood dribbled from the corner of her mouth. She thwacked and kicked, to no avail. His super strength could not be rivalled.

"What are you doing? Let go of me! You're hurting me! Someone, please help me!"

Her pleas went unanswered.

Alpha and Omega stepped forward in unison. Each at the ready. Omega stretched her arms out in front of her and flicked her wrists. A laser beam of frigid air blasted across the room and froze Aurealia's flesh on contact. Webs of ice stretched across her cheeks. Scales emerged through the newly formed cracks in her skin, further betraying her disguise.

Unbearable pain gripped XLV's brain as screams of desperation reverberated around in his cortex. "Now!" he managed.

Divinity slammed his hand down on the console and Tinsler disappeared into a pinpoint of light.

Aurealia's body convulsed violently as it twisted and torqued into impossible positions. Long, razor-like talons grew from her fingertips. Solid black orbs appeared where her eyes once were. A ripple of air ripped across the room. In its wake, the foul smell of sulfur permeated the air. L33t was thrown backwards and released what was once Aurealia. In her place emerged a Tromulite. Before Divinity could react, it bolted at him and speared him in the stomach. Divinity crumpled to the floor. Blood oozed from his wound.

"Noooooo!" screamed Alpha. A wave of anger washed over her. She raised her arms and unleashed a jet stream of fire on the Tromulite. It writhed in agony as its exoskeleton cracked and popped. Steam rose from its eyes and ears. With a thunderous clap, the Tromultie exploded. Blood, bone, and scales spewed in every direction. As the last of the remains splatted on the floor, XLV smashed the teleport button with his fist, and Tinsler reappeared with Aurealia's lifeless body in his arms.

AS XLV APPROACHED THE SICK BAY, A FAMILIAR PURPLE GLOW illuminated the hallway around him. He loved how the blue and red lights calmed his mind. The door to room eleven was open and he could make out Divinity's silhouette sitting beside the bed inside. Before he could announce his presence, Divinity waved him in.

On his way to the bed, XLV grabbed a second chair. He placed it next to Divinity's, sat down and looked at him. "You look exhausted. You need to stop beating yourself up over this. There's no way you could have known that a Tromulite had infiltrated us."

"I should have known. Part of my responsibilities is keeping everyone safe. I failed. When your siblings started dying from the injections, I should have known. I thought there was something wrong with Lot 458. It never occurred to me that the injections were being administered incorrectly... lethally... by an enemy."

"No! A Tromulite killed my siblings. You did NOT!"

"And Aurealia, being trapped in Void that whole time! If Tinsler didn't have super speed, he would never have been able to navigate Void fast enough to get either of them out..." he broke into tears. "And, if you... if you hadn't developed your ability to read minds, we'd all be dead."

"But, we're not. That's all that matters. And now we know that they can shapeshift. We are ahead of their game, once again. We won the battle and we will win the war! Now, please, take a break. I will sit with her for a while."

Reluctantly, Divinity left the room. XLV reached out and took Aurealia's hand in his. He closed his eyes and whispered softly, "Hello, Aurealia. It's XLV. How are you today?"

For the first time, her finger twitched, and a tiny voice responded, *"Hello."*

Rohan's Amazing Adventure

By Sacha Gunaratne

Awake

SPLASH. SCRAPE. SPLASH. SCRAPE. SPLASH. SCRAPE.

I awoke suddenly and tried to stumble up from the tree I had fallen asleep against. I rubbed the sleep from my eyes and scanned the shoreline of the lake in front of me, trying to find the source of the grating noise that woke me from my slumber.

Ugh, I want to get back to the dream where Rani was seductively asking me to follow her into her room.

I had been watching over the lake all my life. I grew up by my father's side; he taught me all he knew. For a moment I let myself get lost in the memory of my father teaching me how to look for shapes under the water by making my eyes slightly unfocused. He was a warrior, who fought off the monster that emerged from the depths to get to the power source that was the lifeblood of the village. The blue glowing object that we referred to as the source, allowed us to cook on the red glowing circles that were hot to touch, preserve food in things called refrigerators, and turned on the lights in the night time. The monster had stopped coming while my father was still alive, yet I watched the water every night, partly in honor of my father who had died from infection after getting cut by a piece of rusted metal, but mostly because the villagers preferred that I stayed away from the main village.

I snapped out of my reverie as I noticed about halfway up the shoreline there was a dark object that seemed to be moving back and forth. I ventured out of my little hidden hut and jogged towards it. The object was a small boat, tied to a tree stump halfway up the beach by a rope. It was being pushed and pulled against the corals on the shore by the waves. In my half-asleep state it took me a moment to recall that nobody in the village had boats.

A cold pit developed in my stomach as I frantically looked around for the tracks of the people who must have come ashore while I was asleep.

Great. Another screw-up on the list of reasons the villagers dislike me.

I saw that there were multiple sets of footprints coming from the boat which headed towards the village. The pit in my stomach turned into a full-blown abyss. I had to warn the village. Since the monsters had gone and we knew there weren't any other villages around us, we had stopped posting guards. If I got there in time, I could save them from whatever fate the men had planned. I would be looked upon favorably again.

Reinvigorated at the thought of redemption and the possibility of being able to sleep in a warm bed again, I ran towards the village but quickly stopped and ran back to the boat. They had gotten past me once, but they weren't going to be able to get away so easily. So, I untied the rope from the tree stump and started to push the boat back into the water. I waded into the water up to about my knees, slowly gaining speed and with a thunderous push sent the boat travelling swiftly into the deeper part of the lake. Satisfied that they couldn't get away I ran back towards the village.

A quarter way down the path to the village which was just a cut pathway through some bushes, I heard a voice, quickly followed by another. The voices had hushed tones and were calm but urgent. I quickly moved off the path and crawled into a pile of leaves trying to make as little noise as possible. It was just in time as the owners of the hushed voices marched by.

There were four of them, I could make out little of their physique in the darkness of the forest, but they looked to be the size of young men. They weren't running which was strange given their urgent tone of voice. As I watched them go by, I stiffened with surprise; a blue glow blinked out from in between the two men in the middle. They had stolen the source.

I stayed still till they passed and slowly got up out of my hiding place dusting off the leaves from my body. I knew that they couldn't escape over the water, so maybe I had time to run back to the village and get help. The villagers would know I wasn't lying since they could see that the source was gone. I hesitated just before my eager legs could break into a spring. If the thieves decided to swim across the lake or hide the source away somewhere, then it would be lost forever. I had to follow them, see where the source ended up and then come back to the village to bring a force of people to get it back. It didn't help that the thought of redemption lingered in the back of my mind.

So once more I headed back up the path towards the lake, treading silently and carefully, trying to catch a glimpse of the dark figures ahead. I could feel every beat of my heart, pulsing the blood through my veins, knowing that I would catch up to them soon.

I reached the beginning of the trail and ducked into the forest that would lead me back to my little hut which gave me a good view of the shoreline. While I was making my way there, I caught glimpses of the four young men on the beach still walking briskly towards the spot where I had found the boat. They hadn't yet noticed that it was gone. It was obvious to me when they did, because the leading man stopped abruptly, and caused the next two men to crash into him. They all nearly lost their balance as the source swung violently in the sack they were carrying it in. I held my breath. Luckily, the last man grabbed the two men before they completely fell over and stopped the source from hitting the ground.

I began moving again and made it to my hidden hut where I watched the four men as they conferred. They seemed to reach a consensus rather quickly because the two men holding the source laid it down while the other ran into the bush and came back with two long straight pieces of wood. They lashed the sack to the pieces of wood and then raised the pieces onto their shoulders carrying the source in between them. The lead man nodded to the other three and then they started off, walking towards Gal Rock, at a quick pace.

Blue blistering barnacles.

I had hoped they would hide the source, leave and return once they somehow figured out how to transport it. But now I was forced to follow them as they walked past Gal Rock into the forest beyond. On second thought, maybe that wouldn't turn out so bad. *Onwards to redemption!*

The Forest

I MADE MY WAY TO GAL ROCK AND PEERED INTO THE FOREST. I COULD just see the dark shapes of their outlines lit up by the light bouncing out of the sack they had tied the source with. They weren't moving fast but kept a steady pace. I steeled myself as I followed the path they made through the brush. The slight breeze muted any noise I made by stepping on leaves or broken branches. They continued in an approximate straight line, almost as if they knew which direction they were travelling in. We hadn't seen people from another village for a long time and it was strange to think that anyone else lived nearby.

I kept my eyes forward as I followed them, keeping my focus on the blue glow to guide me whenever I lost their dark shapes. I crept over logs fallen across the path, pushed small branches out of the way, and swatted away myriad bugs that were attacking my exposed face and arms. In the village we had large storage of mosquito coils that would light up and expel a smoke that would keep them away. I wasn't so lucky now. But I settled into a rhythm as the group in front showed no signs of slowing down.

My legs felt heavy, my breath was ragged, and my mouth was dry. I wish I had brought my water bottle. We must have been moving for a few hours because the sky was starting to brighten. The tinges of dawn were appearing, and the birds were starting to chirp high in the trees. The group had stopped a few times to swap who was carrying the source. It seemed like they chewed on something while they set up the rig on the fresh runners. I couldn't seem to remember the last time I ate food. I used those moments to sit down and massage my calves and try to recuperate. The only thing that kept me going was the thought of bringing the source back to the village. My feet had started to blister; I was not used to travelling for such a long period of time. My life was sedentary, sitting by the lake watching the water where most of the time I was asleep.

I finally saw the group ahead slow down as they approached a large rock face. It was immense, towering up into the sky, from what little I could see through the trees. They moved towards the side of the rock face that was closest to the water and then in a moment, they disappeared. I cursed to myself and stumbled out of the forest, heading towards where I saw them vanish.

As I got closer, I saw it clear as day, an opening in the rock face. I just hadn't been able to see it from where I was. I took one last look around the clearing and entered the opening, crouching a little bit to fit. Slowly I made my way through, it wasn't dark because there was light coming in from the other end. Some dark thoughts of collapsing tunnels crossed my mind, so I quickened my pace towards the end of the tunnel. I could feel a cool, fresh breeze drifting in from the end and I embraced it, breathing in deeply as I exited. I looked around cautiously and that is when I saw the village nestled at the base of the mountain.

The Other Village

I WAS SURPRISED THAT THE VILLAGE HAD BEEN SO CLOSE TO US, HIDDEN in such a way that we had never encountered them or they us. *Except for when they stole the source.* I was trying to figure out the best way to approach the village when I heard a cry of wonderment echo off the walls of the mountain. I saw people moving towards the center of the village, which was designed with the buildings on the outskirts, and a central area which had logs for sitting on. I kept to the trees encompassing the village to get a better vantage point. I saw that quite a few people had made their way out of their huts and were standing around the source. They looked at the source almost reverently and no one was making a move to touch it. Since everyone was distracted by the source, I made my way to the back of one of the village structures. I laid my back against the wooden wall and waited silently to see if anyone had seen me. There were no cries or shouts. It seemed like I had made it there safely. I slowly peeked my head around the corner, and suddenly felt someone grab my shoulder from behind.

I instinctively shrieked and pushed away with my hands. I managed to get the attacker to let go of my shoulder, but I ended up in the corridor between the two houses in plain view of the people. They had heard my scream and turned to look at the commotion.

For a moment everyone was frozen, and then I ran towards them screaming like a wild animal, flailing my hands. None of them moved, or even batted an eyelid. One of the men got up slowly as I made my way towards them at full speed. He walked into my path and just stood there, like a statue. His inaction and complete disregard for the drama I was trying to create completely blew the wind out of my sails and I slowed down and stopped just in front of him. He looked at me quizzically, waiting. I looked up at him, pointed at the source and said, "That's mine, can I have it back?"

He continued to look at me and started nodding slowly as if processing my words. The moment started to stretch out like eternity. It seemed like they didn't speak any English, so I reached for the source. I was startled when he burst into a wide raucous laughter. He turned to the group, and they all started laughing as well. I stopped mid-reach. *Maybe they do speak English after all.*

"Of course, we apologize for our mistake. Please go ahead and take it, " he said as he gestured towards it. So, I reached for it again and he swiftly grabbed my wrist tightly and held fast. I tried to grab at his hand to make him let go but his grip was like steel. I pulled as hard as I could, but he held fast like an old oak. The whole time he smiled, taunting me with his eyes and white, glimmering teeth. I struggled until there was a quieting of the crowd and everyone turned towards something. Or rather, someone. An older man, aged gracefully with lines of wisdom on his face, had emerged from one of the structures. He made his way to the center of the crowd where I struggled to get away from the man with the white teeth.

"Who is this boy?" he asked the man with the white teeth. "He says the puja belongs to him." The older man focused his attention on me. "Is this true boy?"

I thought maybe I had finally reached someone reasonable, so I said, "Yes, it belongs to my village. It is the only thing that allows our village to survive."

He glanced around and said, "Look around, my son, nothing here belongs to anyone. Not anymore." He pointed at the source and said, "But this, this belongs to the gods. And we will deliver it to them." He looked up at the mountain when he said this. He then looked at the man with the gleaming teeth and said, "Make the preparations, we should head up the mountain at once. It has been sometime since we made an offering." With that, he turned away from us and made his way back to his hut.

"What happens now?" I asked the man with the gleaming teeth.

"You can wait here till we offer the puja to the gods. Once it is done, you can go back to where you came from." He dragged me towards one of the huts.

"I'm not just going to wait here without trying to stop you."

He looked at me funny. "Yeah, I know, that's why I'm going to tie you up."

A silent"Oh" left my mouth.

He pulled me into a wooden structure with a thick post in the center of the room. He used a rope to tie my hands behind my back and attached them to the wooden post. He looked out the door and whistled. Soon some footsteps followed and he brought in a young boy.

"This is Sarath." He patted the boy on the shoulder. "He will be looking after you while we go up the mountain." Sarath looked sullenly at me. I returned the sullen look. With that, the man with the gleaming teeth left the hut and Sarath and I were left alone.

"Why are they going up the Mountain?" I asked Sarath. It had been a few hours since I had been tied up. I had heard people gathering outside as they prepared to leave and as they said goodbye to their families. Then they left and the village was quiet again. I had been asking Sarath questions, but he wouldn't answer. He just kept playing with a band of rubber he had in his hand. He kept placing it on his finger and tried to whip it across, but it would always fall at his feet. He seemed to be listening to what I was saying but he just wouldn't respond. Soon after, another boy brought two plates of food into the hut.

He looked at Sarath and said, "You gotta feed him." Sarath scowled at him but he begrudgingly brought over the plate and spoke his first words to me.

"I'm going to feed you, but please behave, otherwise I will have to take the food away."

The smell wafted towards my nose and any thought of escaping left my mind as my stomach took over. I had forgotten how hungry and thirsty I was. I nodded to him. He could see me salivating, so he pulled apart a piece of bread and dipped it in the yellow curry, making a scoop, and brought it to my mouth. I opened my mouth wide and the taste, it was glorious.

I ate ravenously, not caring at all what I looked like. The manners taught to me by my grandmother left by the wayside to be returned to later. Soon Sarath was cleaning the bottom of the bowl with the last remnants of the pieces of bread and I was licking my lips with relief and satisfaction. He pulled a glass from the side of the room and filled it with water from the bucket in the corner and let me sip from it. The fog of hunger and thirst began to lift from my head, and I could feel the life slowly returning to my body. With it returned the aches and pains from the grueling walk the night before. I decided to lean over as much as I could to try and stretch my legs so they wouldn't become stiff. I had a little leeway, so I was able to get some distance over my feet.

Out of nowhere, "Why do you care about the puja so much?" Sarath asked as he continued to play with his band of rubber. I wondered how long he had been waiting to ask me that.

"I'll tell you if you tell me why they are going up the mountain. What are they going to do with it?"

He nodded. "You first."

"Alright, do you know what a refrigerator is? Or a stove top?"

He shook his head. An emphatic no.

"Well, I don't know how they work but if you connect them to the power source..."

He looked at me confused.

"Oh, I mean to the puja then they will keep your food cold or cook your food for you."

His eyes lit up. "Oh, like fire!"

I shook my head. "I haven't heard of that."

He seemed surprised. "Why did your village send you? You're not a talented fighter" he said after a brief pause.

I laughed heartily at that, which prompted a look of frustration from Sarath. "They didn't send me. I wanted to get it back myself." Sarath still had a look of confusion on his face. "Alright, fine. I'll tell you." I sighed with resignation. "I was sort of planning an elaborate prank on a friend of mine and everything was going well, but one of the village elders happened to walk into the vicinity, and well, he had a heart attack and died in my arms."

"Woah. That sucks." he seemed genuinely empathetic. "Wait, what was the prank?" he asked, his voice tinged with curiosity.

"It's a long story." I said shaking my head. Sarath looked eager to hear more but I changed topics "You know, the source also lets you become very strong and fly around but you have to use this special key that I have around my neck." I gestured towards my neck using my head. He seemed intrigued so I said, "Here come take a look at it." He walked over and pulled my shirt down. I immediately lifted my hips up and grabbed his midsection between my thighs and started to squeeze. He tried to grab at my face, but I held fast. I was so focused on him that I didn't notice the boy from earlier rush into the hut and pull him free. He then thundered over and slapped me. Hard.

Sarath was lying on the floor, dazed and gasping for air. The other boy was shouting at me, but my ears were ringing. Sarath called out something and he stopped. He looked back and I heard him say"Are you sure?"

"Yeah, they've been gone long enough, he'll never catch them. And anyway, I can't be bothered watching him anymore." Sarath said while looking at me with annoyance. The other boy went behind the pole and untied my hands. "Go on, you clearly care a lot about your-" he paused"-source" Sarath gulped as he said it.

He gestured to the door. I didn't need to be told twice. I ran out, turned towards the mountain trail and headed up the looming facade.

The Mountain and the Gods

THE PATH UP THE MOUNTAIN WAS WINDY BUT CLEAR. I SAW QUITE FAR ahead but there was no sign of the procession carrying the source. I had some catching up to do. I ran up the pathway, but quickly realized that I was not prepared to do that for more than a few moments at a time. So, I slowed down my pace but kept it consistent as I moved up the mountain path. My calves started to burn almost immediately, the feeling traveling up my leg towards my thigh and buttocks. I gritted my teeth and kept going, trying to keep my mind off the pain. I focused on the idea of rescuing the source and reveled in the daydream of fighting them off with a stick while I danced around like a battle-hardened veteran. I could imagine my triumphant return to my village, power source held high in my hands as everyone cheered and clapped. I would spin tales of valor and fear, of the time I got captured but managed to escape by talking my way out of the confines of my cell with my smooth words, of the time I fought off the villagers at the top of the mountain where the source was the only witness, and of the time I saved a young damsel from being crushed by a boulder.

I was pulled out of my daydream by a twinge in my leg. I stopped for a moment and bent at the waist, completely out of breath as I gasped to fill my lungs with the thin mountain air. The village down below looked small. I heaved for enough breath and stood up straight to peer further up the mountain path, but I couldn't see anything yet. I had to keep moving, otherwise all this would have been for nothing. So, I started again, one foot in front of the other, making sure to focus only on the placement of my feet and not on the task at hand. I slowly started to increase my pace while I got into a rhythm. I felt it energize me. It was then that I realized that I was walking to a beat. A beat sounding off from the top of the mountain. It was faint but it was there, if you listened hard enough. I was close. It spurred me on to start running, and I blasted up the mountain path towards my fate.

I crept up the path as I got closer to the source of the noise. I moved to the left side of the path and entered the forest. I started to see the villagers gathered. Surprisingly, there was a large body of water up on the mountain. The water was crystal clear and shone brightly in the afternoon sun. It was mesmerizing. I was reminded of my task as I saw the villagers remove the source from the sack and place it on an altar of rock. It glowed dully, outclassed by the blue water behind it. The villagers continued to chant and beat their drums. The beat started to get faster and faster. The hands of the drummers moving in unison, as they got progressively louder. Beads of sweat glistened off their foreheads as they worked their drums. The chants reached a fever pitch and just when you thought they had reached their crescendo they kept going, holding the intense pitch and beat until they all slowly dropped off one at a time until there was only one man left. He brought the pitch down and slowly reduced his volume until finally, he grew silent and let the echoes of their chants and drums bounce around the valley that hid this lake. Everything was silent. The villagers all slowly turned to face the lake. *This was my chance.*

As soon as I started to move towards them, there was a rumbling. Almost a low hum, a vibration of sorts. The villagers stepped back. Some slowly, others jerkily so. I felt that familiar pit in my stomach as the water rippled and a shape emerged. It moved erratically out of the water and in the afternoon light, I saw the monster clearly for the first time in my life. The monster that my father had protected our village from. He had described it in perfect detail; The dull metal encompassing it, the lush vines and dense organic material that seemed to grow out of the crevices and the haunting groans that it emitted when it moved.

It moved out of the water onto the rocky shore. The villagers just watched it, I could tell the ones that had seen the monster before from the ones that hadn't. They, like me, were struggling to keep their mouths from falling open. I watched transfixed as the monster extended one of its metallic arms and pinched the power source. It grabbed it swiftly and maneuvered it into a slot that opened on its back. My shoulders drooped as the air whooshed from my lungs and I dropped to the floor. *How am I going to get it back now?* I couldn't fight that thing. I wasn't my father. I wasn't a warrior. While I was thinking about what to do, the monster turned and swiftly submerged itself into the waters of the mountain lake. The only evidence that it had ever been up there were in the little waves that began to hit the shore.

The villagers waited a moment and then began to leave, chatting amongst each other, and joking about who would have been able to fight the monster better, and who would have run away screaming back down the mountain. I waited for them to leave and walked out to the altar at the lake. It was a simple design, two rocks placed on top of each other. I picked up a small, flat rock and threw it into the lake, trying to skip it. I counted the skips before the rock plunged into the depths. Twenty-five. *At least I can still skip stones.*

I walked back towards the main path when I heard a now familiar rumble. The deep thrum coming from the water. I ran back into the bushes. *This is becoming a common occurrence - me in the bushes.* I watched as the monster emerged from the water once more. It's dull metal gleaming in the evening light. It stopped near the altar and there was a hiss, and the face of the monster opened and a blond pale man stood up from within and slowly began to climb down the body.

He got off and stood next to the altar. He seemed like he was thinking about something and then he started to urinate on the altar. Out of the corner of my eye, I noticed movement. It was another man, pale like the first. He appeared from the far side of the lake, near the edge of the mountain. The urinating man acknowledged the second man and they started speaking to each other. I couldn't understand what they were saying.

"Ah, Johan, wie gehts?"

"Bis gut. Und du Friedrich?"

"Alas Klar. Noch Einer ah."

"Ja, aber sie werden immer seltener. Ich wiess nicht, wie lange wir dort unten bleiben werden."

This was finally my moment, while they were talking. I needed a weapon. I looked around for a stick that would be sturdy, and I could hit someone with. *Everything is too long!*

I had no choice but to snap it to size. I grabbed a sturdy, long stick, and pulled one side gently, while I put my leg in the middle. It was bending and just when I thought I had gotten past the cracking sound, it snapped with a loud crack.

The two men stopped speaking and turned to investigate the trees. I tried to stay as still as possible, all thoughts of my attack gone. They looked around and then resumed talking. I took a few deep breaths, trying to pump myself up to go face them. I grabbed my stick and emerged from the trees and started making my way towards them, holding my stick out and trying to be as menacing as possible.

"Arghhh, " I growled. They turned to look at me in surprise. "Give me back my power source, " I exclaimed loudly.

"I forgot people up here still speak English, " said the man who urinated on the altar in a funny voice.

His response made me pause. I hadn't expected them to speak to me in English. *I should assume everyone speaks English after what happened in the village.*

He looked at me with pity. "Do you mean the fusion core?" he asked.

"We call it the source, " I said emphatically.

"Unfortunately, we need it. There are a bunch of scientists and families in an underwater bunker that need the fusion core to power the water-to-oxygen converter and keep the lights on so the scientists can finish working on the large-scale fusion reactors to power the underwater ships and bring the entire civilization down there back onto land."

I didn't understand most of what he said. *There are people who were living underwater? How do they breathe?* These were questions for another time. Instead, I swung the stick hard and fast, emulating my father.

The men reacted easily, like I was swinging the stick at a snail's pace. The man who had urinated stepped to the side, grabbed the stick on the downswing and pulled hard. I was off balance and tripped forward and landed on the ground with my palms out to break my fall. I saw the feet of the men move quickly after that, as I lay dazed on the ground.

"Bis spater." The pale man jumped back in the monster and with a hiss, the monster's face was back on and he descended into the water one last time.

The Return

AFTER WAITING FOR THE OTHER PALE MAN TO WALK TOWARDS THE FAR side of the lake, I got up and dusted myself off. My palms were stinging from the fall. I rubbed them against my legs to try and relieve the pain. I took one last look at the water, and headed down the mountain path, with the evening sun to guide me. The downhill path took me a lot less time than before. I don't know if it was the fact that I was going down, or whether I was relieved that my journey home was beginning. I made it past the spot that I started to hear the beat of the drums, and where I had stopped gasping for air. It soon got to the point where I could see the village down below. I felt a sensation at the back of my neck from looking down there. It was faint, but in the evening shadows, there was light coming from the village. I remembered the village leader saying that they didn't have any power sources. *How is there light?*

I quickened my pace, excitement growing. The hair stood up on the back of my neck. I ran into the village at full tilt until I reached the men and women gathered around the beautifully glowing, vibrant light that was somehow warm. I couldn't keep my eyes off it. The way it danced and crackled.

Most people were staring at me, so I asked, "What is this? What is this magical thing?"

"It's called fire, " said Sarath who I hadn't noticed sitting on the side. He motioned for me to come and sit next to him. "I can show you how to make it, " he said.

My face broke into a huge grin. "I can make this?"

"Any time you want." He said something about rubbing two sticks together.

I waved him off and said, "Show me later, I just want to watch the fire." My face was tired from smiling. Sarath brought over some food, and I ate it, savoring every bite and enjoying the warmth of the fire with the knowledge that we didn't need the power source anymore.

I hung around the village by the mountain till the next day and then began my trek back through the forest. It was a lot easier to get through because it was day time, and I was able to follow the route along the edge of the lake. I walked at a leisurely pace, thinking up what I would tell the villagers. I would tell them I saw the monster and that it took the source, and then when all hope was lost, I would reveal fire and light up everyone's mood. By the time I got back to Gal rock it was starting to get dark. So, I sped up my walk hoping to show them the fire before it got too dark out, because they didn't have the source anymore. As I made it to the village, I saw something that sent a shiver up my spine. There was light coming from the village. *No effing way.* I sprinted into the village.

"Where have you been Rohan?" asked my grandmother, who was tending to a pot by the fire. I was dumbfounded, my hopes of saving the village slowly starting to fade away. "Someone came and stole the power source while you were gone, " she said.

I nodded dumbly. "Uh, I was by the water. I haven't seen anyone for days." I said as I sat down in front of the fire.

"This is fire, " she said pointing to the fire. "It is how we used to cook in the old days."

Without thinking I said, "I know." She looked at me surprised. I quickly followed it up with, "I must have seen in a book somewhere." She nodded placated with my answer for now. I knew I'd hear about it later.

I reached over to warm my hands over the dancing flame and the cuts on my palms burned reminding me of my absolute failure over the last few days. *This is what I get for trying.*

Tattoos Of Water And Ice

By Ainslee Gagné

"HEY GUYS, LOOK, IT'S THAT WEIRD, WHITE-HAIRED KID, " SOME random student whispers as they pass Xavier. Xavier lets out a silent yawn and ignores them as his teacher rambles on about elven geography, specifically stuff everyone already knows. His gaze drifts outside as he grows bored.

"Mr. Moon, does my teaching bore you?" the teacher asks and Xavier's gaze snaps back to the teacher in an instant, his face turning red.

"I-I'm sorry. Of course I'm not, I just th-thought I saw something outside..." he stutters and the teacher smirks at him before turning back to the class. Xavier sinks down in his seat, embarrassed. He hates being put in the spotlight.

His white hair falls into his eyes and he brushes it out of the way. His hair really needs a trim, it now reaches just below his eyes and gets in the way a lot, which annoys him. Hair has always been a problem in his life, first it being snow white, next it being too long, and now it just draws attention.

The bell rings in the hallway and everyone quickly stands to leave. It's finally the weekend, everyone is free from school. Xavier puts up his hood and walks out, avoiding everyone's gazes. It takes about 15 minutes for Xavier to get home, and as soon as he gets home, he tosses his bag on the floor next to his bed. The bed creaks as he sits on it, and he stares at his school bag, contemplating whether or not to do his homework about the King and Queen. Ultimately, he shrugs and lays down, deciding to nap and then do his homework later in the afternoon. As soon as his head hits the pillow, he passes out.

XAVIER AWAKES WITH A STRETCH AND DREARILY TOSSES THE BLANKETS to the side. He half stumbles to the bathroom, starting his morning routine. He'd overslept and forgotten to do his homework as he'd planned. That's annoying, he'll now have homework to do over the weekend. The light turns on and he squints his eyes. He gets his toothbrush ready and begins to brush his teeth. Once his eyes become used to the light, he opens them fully. He freezes and his toothbrush falls from his hand. Xavier's eyes widen on his reflection in the mirror and his jaw drops. Swirling black tattoos flow across his entire torso. There doesn't seem to be any picture formed by them, they just swirl like water over his skin.

In a panic he throws on a shirt and quietly opens his bedroom door. His parents aren't awake yet, and he's surprisingly happy about that. The thought of explaining these tattoos to his parents frightened him, so this makes life easier. Thankfully his little brother and sister are also still asleep, he doesn't want to have to deal with taking care of them during this mess. His stomach growls hungrily, guess he'll have to make himself breakfast. Not one light in the house is turned on, which gives off a creepy vibe that he doesn't like, so he rushes to turn on the lights. Thankfully, there was nothing waiting for him in the darkness, so he continues on making himself a breakfast.

Still slightly groggy from getting up, he turns on the tap to get himself some cold water. The glass in his hand grows cold as the water fills it up, but it becomes so unbearably cold that he nearly drops it. He stares at in confusion. It's completely frozen, not one drop of liquid water is left.

Panic once again builds in his mind, first the tattoos and now this? What is going on? He attempts to get another glass, but this time the water changes direction and splashes onto his face. His hand quickly wipes away the water as the doorbell rings. Internally he yells in a panicked frenzy, hoping nobody would accidentally mistake him as one of the many gang members in the city, since they all possess tattoos. Almost no normal citizens have tattoos unless they are in a gang, it doesn't help that you can see the tattoo just peeking over the collar of his shirt. The door swings open with a swift movement on his hand and he attempts to act normal, all the while being drenched.

IN FRONT OF XAVIER STANDS A WOMAN ELF. SHE IS DRESSED IN ALL black, even sporting black hair, and has a tattoo just under her right eye. The tattoo is a small lotus flower. Mystery envelopes her as she smirks, taking a small step forward. What does this woman want? Time freezes as he suddenly recognizes the small tattoo, it's a gang tattoo.

The Lotus gang is one of the most notorious gangs in this city. What is one of them doing at his front door? He slams the door in her face, and he observes her mouth part in slight surprise before it shuts. Xavier decides that the best thing he can possibly do in the moment is run. If one of them is there, there are most likely more of them waiting. To protect his family, he must run away, at least temporarily.

Lights flicker on in his parents' room as he puts on his jacket, stuffs some food in a bag and slips on his shoes. Before his parents can exit their room, Xavier opens the back door and breaks into a sprint. The nearest bus stop is about seven-hundred meters away, so he runs as fast as he can.

Behind him he can hear fast footsteps, obviously chasing him. This just pushes Xavier to run faster. The other elf doesn't let up once in the chase. What is he going to do if the bus isn't there? It isn't like he can just stop at the bus stop and wait with this woman chasing him. Up ahead he can see a bus, pulling up to the stop. With all of his remaining power he runs into the bus just as the doors shut. A glance out the window proves he was right about her chasing him, as she is standing at the bus stop, looking frustrated. Xavier plops himself down on a free seat and takes deep breaths, still recovering from the long sprint and panic he's feeling.

XAVIER LOOKS AROUND AFTER STEPPING OFF THE BUS IN A QUIET AREA of the city, trying to figure out where he is. To his left he spots a library, which immediately sparks an idea in his head. Maybe the library will hold some answers regarding his tattoos. Once inside, he scans all the signs that give the genre of each section in the library. He figures that elven history would be the best place to start. Soon enough he finds a book titled"The Tattoos", which is very relevant to his current situation. Apparently, every fifty years, a group of young elves wake up with tattoos, each with their own corresponding powers. He wonders if the King and Queen know of this, it's a pretty big deal. Maybe they've never been informed, since no one Xavier's ever known has mentioned it. It doesn't give any clues as to why it happens, but it confirms that there are two elves in every city affected by it. This gives Xavier hope that he isn't completely alone, but he lives in one of the biggest cities on the continent, the probability of him finding the other elf is very low. With a sigh he places the book back on the shelf and exits the library.

THE SUN IS NOW HALFWAY THROUGH THE SKY, THE BRIGHTEST TIME OF the day. Behind him he hears a piercing scream. His head whips around and he sees a girl he recognizes as an elf running away from another dressed in dark clothes. Her light brown hair bounces wildly around her head as she runs as fast as she can. Xavier quickly realizes that the elf chasing her is another member of the Lotus gang. At this realization, he turns and runs after the girl. She almost leaves his sight, but the yells of people telling her to slow down up ahead keep him with a general idea of where she is. When she's back in his sight, he speeds up and grabs her arm, pulling her into an alleyway. They duck behind a garbage can and watch as the other elf, this time a man, runs by.

The girl yanks her arm away from his grip and they both stand. "Thanks for saving me, but next time give a warning please, " she says as she rubs her forearm. Xavier shifts his weight between his feet nervously, not used to talking to other people. Now he must put up a calm front, pretending this is normal and not panicking, for everyone's sake.

"Sorry. I was also being chased earlier by a member of the same gang. Do you have any idea why they're after you?" he inquires.

She shakes her head, which makes her hair fall over her face. As she reaches up to brush it out of the way her sleeve falls down, revealing lightning bolt tattoos. "Hey nice tattoos, " he compliments, "did you wake up with those?"

"How did you know?"

"I woke up with tattoos on my torso this morning, " Xavier explains, "and I went to the library to try to figure out why this is happening. One of the books says there are two elves affected in each city."

"So, I guess we're the two elves. Did the book say why this is happening?" she asks hopefully.

"Nope, it's weird. It had everything except that."

"But it says there are two elves affected in each city, which means there's more of us in the other cities, we should try to find them!" she exclaims.

"You're right, that would be our best hope at getting answers about the tattoos and the elves chasing us, but this is a big decision, can you give me a second to think please?" he requests. The girl nods and lets the conversation pause for a bit.

This is a huge decision, but he knows he doesn't have much of a choice with the Lotus gang on their tail. He doesn't even know this girl! Going to a different city with a complete stranger is pretty crazy, especially compared to his quiet life. Xavier does know his way around, having grown up with parents who love to travel, but it's quite sudden. By now his parents would be beginning to worry, should he call them? No, then the gang would associate them together, he doesn't want to put his family at risk. His mind is saying it's crazy, but he knows he has to go.

"All right, I'll come with you to find the others, " he eventually agrees.

"Hey, I forgot to ask, what's your name?"

"Oh, I'm Xavier, " Xavier greets and puts out his hand.

She happily grabs his hand and shakes it. "Nice to meet you Xavier, I'm Aurora."

THE TWO GANG MEMBERS, ALSO KNOWN AS THE LOTUS PETALS, GROW frustrated. Evie, the Lotus gang's leader, calls Zephon, her second in command, to inform him that her target got away on the bus. Zephon proceeds to tell her that his target got away too. Evie lets out a frustrated sigh and they decide to meet up on the corner of a busy street. She adjusts her black leather jacket and gets onto the next bus. How did she let him get away? It was such a simple chase yet the stupid white-haired boy escaped. It takes about 15 minutes to get to the street corner, and when she does, Zephon is already waiting for her. She raises her hand in greeting and they sit down on a bench next to each other.

"So, what does your target look like?" Zephon asks.

"He's taller than both of us, slim but still strong and his most outstanding feature is his snow-white hair. He's pretty easily noticeable, but his tattoos are on his torso so they aren't what we can use to recognize him, since they'll be hidden by a shirt, " Evie briefly explains.

"Mine is quite short, she has long light brown hair and if you look at her face her most recognizable feature is her heterochromia, one eye blue and one eye yellow. Her tattoos are on her right arm, so they're noticeable if she wears short sleeves. If she's smart she'll cover her arms, " Zephon summarizes, "we are quite lucky the gang boss got that new censor. Though he still hasn't told us how it functions in a detailed way, I know it can sense when magic is in use and where."

"Yes, we are lucky, this makes it a lot easier, rather than trying to find out who they are and get pictures of them with nothing to go off of. This isn't the time to be happy though, if we don't capture those two elves, Boss is going to kill us. They are very important for his next big move in the Mafia world. He's not going to be happy if we can't capture them, especially if the other gangs he's paid off in the other cities capture their targets, " Evie sighs.

"I'm sure we'll be fine Evie, if they all got magic, then why would Boss need all of them for his experiments?"

"Zephon, you idiot, they all have different powers, he wants all of them."

"Does he really need all of them to overthrow the King and Queen?" Zephon asks a little too loudly and a few heads turn in their direction.

"Shut up! Don't say such things out in the open for anyone to hear!"

"Let's split up and try to find them. Call me when you find them, " Evie bids farewell as Zephon stands and sprints away.

Evie stands as well and begins wandering the city. After all of these years, never once has Boss ever messed with these magically gifted elves. Not one person in the mafia knows where his idea came from, but one day he showed up and started informing us of them. He bought some new technology that can sense when magic is in use, and since then all his focus has been on finding them. Apparently, the sole reason he chose this time to find them is because he finally had the tech to experiment on their magic with. After about ten minutes of wandering, something catches her eye. A tall elf with snow white hair and a short elf with long light brown hair are getting onto a bus that leads towards the train station. That's when it clicks in her mind, they're going to attempt to find the others! Her phone is immediately in hand, calling Zephon. "They are going to leave the city on the train! Get to the train station ASAP!" she shouts before hanging up.

Her legs move before her brain can even think of what to do. She's sprinting full speed, towards the train station, wasting no time trying to hail a taxi or wait for the next bus. By the time she arrives she's out of breath, but the train hasn't left yet, and their bus hasn't arrived. She whispers a silent thanks for her heightened elven speed. She has been known for having wonderful endurance since she was young, and has continued to improve since, so she is a fantastic runner. The bus probably has a few stops and detours left before getting here. The only thing that Evie can think of doing to stop the train is to destroy the engine. How? She has no clue, but it will create an explosion, so she will have to be quick enough to get out and shout at the others to move away before it goes kaboom. Her heart aches a little for the injured, since they are just innocent bystanders. She may be a gang leader, but she most definitely isn't heartless, and she never has been. Evie prefers to stick to her targets, and just her targets, when it comes to harming anyone, since the majority of them have done something wrong to her or the gang boss.

One of the train doors are open for the staff to come and go, so she has to sneak inside. A few security guards pace back and forth around the train, so she has to time it perfectly. Once the security guards are all facing away from the entrance she runs inside. It doesn't take her long to find the engine room, but there are even more people around. They are all dressed in casual clothes, so all she has to do is act like she belongs there. With confidence she strolls right through the group of staff and into the engine room, none of them even suspected her. Inside it's quite uncomfortably warm but she pushes through the warmth and grabs a metal pipe. It was probably there in case the mechanics had to replace something. She brings the pipe over her head and smashes it down on the engine with all of her strength. After repeating the process over and over again the engine begins to make some weird noises and a small fire erupts inside. The room heats up even more and she swings open the door screaming at everyone in sight to run. She leaps off of the train and keeps shouting, until a large blast sounds behind her. A few people scream and others call the royal guard. In a matter of minutes, the guard arrives and begins investigating. They announce the closure of city borders and Evie smiles contently. Those two elves aren't going anywhere on her watch.

WHEN XAVIER AND AURORA HEAR THE NEWS OF THE BORDER CLOSURE, they panic. The bus takes them back to where they were picked up. Aurora brings Xavier to a small cafe close to the border of the city. Once there, they sit down on a sofa, feeling thankful for the break from running. "Xavier, we need to get out of this city, " Aurora starts, "but our only way of legally and safely leaving this city has been taken away."

"I know, Aurora. Maybe we'll have to leave illegally. We could try to sneak out."

"We'll get caught if we just sneak out, maybe we should disguise ourselves as part of the royal guard?"

"Ya, that could work, but how would we disguise ourselves. We don't have uniforms, " he points out.

"Hm, I guess so. Since we're here, I'm going to go get a drink, do you want anything?" she offers.

"I'll have water, thanks." Aurora nods and gets up to ask the barista for their drinks. The barista happily takes her order and gives her the drinks. Aurora hands Xavier the glass of water and sets her coffee down on the coffee table in front of them. Seeing the water reminds Xavier of what happened that morning. He glances at the glass of water and gets an idea.

"Hey Aurora, something weird happened to me this morning. Look at this." She pays attention as Xavier places his hands on the glass, picturing what happened that morning. He imagines the water freezing and feels the glass go uncomfortably cold.

Aurora lets out a small gasp as the water freezes into a solid block of ice. "What is that?" she asks.

"I don't know. I woke up with these tattoos and this happened when I got myself water this morning."

"Weird, they must be connected."

"Well, in the book I read earlier, it said that we wake up with tattoos and powers, " he explains.

"Oh, I wonder what my power is, " Aurora comments as she goes to plug in her phone. She plugs it in and Xavier watches as a bolt of electricity shoots from the outlet and straight into Aurora. She doesn't even shout, as if nothing harmed her, but her eyes are wide, and her mouth is hanging open. They meet eyes and laughter erupts from her as she falls to the ground, gasping for air. Xavier joins in eventually, laughing just as much as her.

In just a few seconds, sirens sound outside and car doors slam. Aurora and Xavier stand immediately, prepared to run.

Xavier glances at the barista, who has a phone in his hand. "I'm sorry, you were s-scaring me, " he whispers.

The royal guard slam open the cafe doors and they take off. Aurora and he exit through the back door and run without abandon towards the city border.

They stumble upon a wide river. He had heard the water a little while back while they were running and had begun to plan. He knows that he has the capability to freeze water, but can he freeze water at such a large scale? He thinks back to when he was uselessly freezing water in the cup. When he had done that, he had pictured the cup freezing in his mind. Maybe, just maybe, he could picture the water freezing under him as they ran across the lake, and it would obey his thoughts? It's the only hope he has. Without stopping, Xavier runs straight onto the river, freezing it beneath him. Aurora runs behind him, trying not to slip and fall, as the ice melts about three feet behind her. Once across, they run into the forest and stop with their backs against trees. It has become dark out, and up ahead a small fire peeps between the trees. "Xavier, let's go towards the fire, it's our best bet. Maybe it's others that have run away like us."

SIX PEOPLE ARE SITTING AROUND THE FIRE, SOME WITH TATTOOS blatantly shown, and some with no apparent tattoos. Xavier and Aurora approach them cautiously. *What if they aren't our friends? What if they are part of a gang?* The aura surrounding them doesn't seem violent, if anything he feels drawn to them.

Aurora pulls up her sleeve, exposing her tattoos. Of course, Xavier wasn't about to take off his shirt in front of a bunch of strangers just to expose his tattoos, so he just follows along behind Aurora. The group of people look at the two newcomers and a few of them stand, seemingly ready to fight. They observe Xavier and Aurora closely, scrutinizing every little thing just make sure they are friendly. Their expressions change from intimidating to friendly within seconds.

"You must be the two elves from this city, my name's James, " a tall and strong elf greets.

"Hello! My name's Aurora and this is Xavier. How come you guys are camping out here?" she asks.

"We are all being chased by different gangs, I assume you are as well, so we left the cities to try to hide from them. My name is Issac, " another elf introduces himself.

"So, we can trust you?" Xavier finally speaks up, overcoming his nervousness.

"Yes, we have all been through the same thing."

"How long have you guys been out here?" Aurora inquires.

"We all came at different times throughout the year, me and Alice have been here the longest, " James explains. They all follow him back to the group and introduce themselves.

From what Xavier gathers, the leaders of the group are James, who has fire powers, and Alice, who can bend metal. A sort of power couple. Issac has control over the air and Rose can heal others' wounds. The other two, Kai and Annabelle, have control over weather and plants respectively.

"So, we've all been chased by different gangs?" Rose asks with a soft-spoken voice.

"So it seems, and that could mean they've all been paid off by the same person, right?" Alice inquires.

"The only person that I can think of as powerful enough to do that is the gang boss, what would he want from us? We've done nothing wrong! It's not our fault we have these tattoos and powers!" Annabelle complains.

"Annabelle, I get that this isn't a good situation, but could you please hold off on the complaining, " James asks in an ordering tone. Annabelle just rolls her eyes at him.

"She is right though, it would make the most sense for it to be the gang boss, " Aurora chimes in.

"But what would his motives be?" Xavier questions.

"The gang boss's motives for everything have always been a mystery to everyone except for his closest peers, " James explains.

"So then we all agree that it's most likely the gang boss? I've heard that he takes residence in our city, " Aurora says.

"Well than shouldn't we go into the city?" Xavier asks.

"I think that would be the best course of action, " Kai finally speaks.

"Well, if everyone is on the same page, let's go back to my house! My parents are away for the weekend, they told me no parties, I'm sure this isn't the type of party they meant, " Aurora jokes.

"There is no party, Aurora, " James says.

"Are you kidding me? Whenever a group of teenagers this big get together, it's a party!"

They cross the river again and Aurora leads them to her house. Xavier puts up his hood, concealing his white hair from view.

Once at Aurora's house, they all sit down and wait, knowing that the lotus gang members will come eventually. Luckily for them, the gang members show up fairly soon. James and Kai sit near the window, while

Issac is next to the front door. The two gang members for some reason thought it was a good idea to crash through the window.

Glass shards go flying around the room, and Xavier lifts his arm to protect his face. While his eyes are covered, he hears some loud thumping and some noises that sound like fighting. By the time Xavier uncovers his eyes, James and Kai have both gang members captured, with their hands behind their backs. Kai has a nasty bruise blooming on his cheek and James' lip is split and bleeding. Alice steps forward menacingly. "Tell us where the gang boss is."

"Why would we tell you that, we aren't idiots, " the girl snarls.

"We have complete reason to call the royal guard right now if you don't tell us, " Alice threatens.

"Evie, maybe we should tell them, " the boy whispers.

"Shut up, Zephon, let me deal with this, " Evie retorts.

"What's your decision?" Alice persists.

"Fine, the gang boss is in a penthouse downtown. The address is 2470 Silver Lane, " Evie gives in.

"Alright guys, let's head out, " Alice says and they all follow her out of the house.

"Wait, I don't want to be responsible for any deaths, okay? The building has heavy security. You'll have to break in, " Evie warns as everyone leaves.

"So are we going to stop them?" Zephon asks.

"Well, I don't think it would be a good idea to get involved, since the gangs are most likely going to be arrested, " she says while standing. The two of them are stuck in a predicament. Go and be arrested or stay safe and ignore the fight. She looks around and notices that when the gifted elves left the locked everything. They are stuck, with no way to get out.

Evie was right, as the group approaches the building, they see many cameras and guards. James sends Issac and Kai around back, hoping to find a back entrance. Xavier and Aurora stick together, unconsciously used to being a team. Kai and Issac run back towards them and Xavier listens to their feedback. Apparently, there is a door, and it's not too heavily guarded, but they'll still have to fight. Everyone agrees that's inevitable and they'll head to the door Kai and Isaac found.

Xavier trails along behind Aurora as they enter the building. Once again, Xavier is panicking inside, going over all the possible outcomes of the fight. He doesn't show it, but he really wants to just turn and run. With his newfound control over water, he is just a tiny bit more confident, but he still isn't comfortable in this situation. They all crowd around the elevator and wait but Xavier notices a staircase. Without speaking he makes the gesture for them to follow, which they do. James takes the lead once again, Xavier not wanting to take that position. Xavier definitely doesn't want to take the role of leader, with the building panic inside of him, he'd be a horrible role model for everyone else.

After climbing up twelve flights of stairs, they encounter a metal door with a keyhole. Alice steps forward and places her hands on the door. The door seems to become liquid metal that she controls. It melts around her hands and she creates an opening wide enough for all of them to fit through. Once through, even more stairs await, so they climb up another five flights of stairs. Xavier begins to get anxious, realizing that they were about to enter the biggest gang boss's lair. This is the most dangerous thing he's ever done.

With a deep sigh he continues climbing. At the top of the seemingly never-ending stairs is another door, this time with a keypad. Aurora places her hand on the keypad and electricity sparks around it before they hear a click. Xavier pauses, along with the rest of the group as the door swings open. It's a large room with high ceilings, a throne-like seat sits at the front of a large table. Surrounding that table are 10 gang leaders and many of their guards. It all happens in a flash. James shouts at Issac to create an air shield around them as fire erupts around the room. Xavier looks around and notices that everyone else is occupied with other gang members.

To his left, he spots the gang boss trying to escape through a side door in the wall opposite to his seat. The aura surrounding the boss was very scary, and his dark mysterious clothing doesn't help. The man is well built, definitely stronger than Xavier, and his face holds an expression of anger and shock. Xavier opens his bottle of water and the water flies out. He imagines it becoming hard and hitting his head with just enough force to knock him out. The water does exactly as he imagined, and the gang boss gets knocked out. The majority of the gang has either passed out from lack of oxygen or been knocked out, so Issac clears out the air shield. Xavier notices his friends turn their backs to the gang boss and chat, not even sparing a glance towards the knocked-out gang boss. In the corner of his eye Xavier spots movement. Two stray gang members had run over and have begun to carry the gang boss away. Issac quickly notices and prevents them from breathing just long enough for them to pass out. Xavier notices a sharp pain in his arm and looks down to see a cut. Someone must have thrown a dagger at him in the midst of the fight. Blood seeps into his sleeve and he hisses in pain. He quickly clutched his arm, putting pressure on the cut, trying to stop the bleeding. "Hey Rose, do you mind healing this please?" he asks politely.

"Of course, " she smiles and places her hand over the cut. His skin feels a warm tingly sensation and when she retracts her hands the wound is completely healed. Rose quickly moves on to all of the others' wounds, placing her hands on them. Annabelle calls the royal guard and they all sit to wait, not wanting to leave the gang on its own. Once the royal guard arrives, they all relax and they get sent home.

Xavier enters his home to find many warm hugs waiting for him. His heart swells with joy at the thought of his family being safe. Although, how he's going to live his life normally from now on is a great question. His mom pulls back and grabs his face in her hands. "So, you're an elf? Why didn't you tell us this! We thought you had gotten mixed in with the wrong crowd after that Lotus gang girl stopped by looking for you!" his mother rants.

"I'm sorry mom, I only wanted to keep you safe."

"Dear, we are always here for you, please don't hide such a huge thing from us again."

"Thank you, mom, I won't."

With the tattoos and his gift not going away anytime soon, people may be afraid of him. He doesn't like attention, but he doesn't feel as lonely as before. Finding a group of people like him, who accept him, warms his heart. His self-consciousness has dropped drastically since he left home, and he now sports his white hair proudly. His head hits the pillow and he yawns, happy he can sleep safely in his own bed without bringing danger to his family. While he was out with Aurora and the rest of the group, he didn't know when he'd be able to return, two days passed by so fast. The royal guard are most likely going to come by tomorrow and interrogate him, but besides that, everything seems normal. Until Xavier's mom runs into his room holding some sort of letter. She hands it to him, completely speechless. Inside the letter reads:

Dear Xavier Moon,

Thank you for aiding us in capturing the gang boss of this land. We were aware of his presence in your city but could never get any information on his exact location. Until you and your group of gifted elves came along. Your leaders, James and Alice, didn't want to take all the credit, so they informed us of all of everyone's hard work. Also, that you, specifically, were the one to capture the gang boss. It's unimaginable that a 17-year-old boy would go through such a thing. So thank you for you work, you are truly appreciated. We hope you can return to your normal life and cherish your new friends.

Best regards,
The King and Queen

Xavier looks up slowly, trying to process the letter. The King and Queen sent him a letter? How is such a thing possible? His mother looks at him proudly and gives him another big hug. "You've made everyone proud, my boy, even the King and Queen, " his father says as he enters the room. Xavier's father gives him another hug and his mom joins in. Soon his brother and sister run in and jump into the group hug. A hug he will cherish for the rest of his life, hoping that the future will turn out just as he plans; normal. But with all that has changed, that idea doesn't hold up for very long.

Children of Newton

By K. W. Nyhuus

1

YOU THINK YOU KNOW THE STORY OF THOMAS HARRY JENSON. BUT you don't.

So, let me summarize.

Thomas Harry Jenson is the man destined to be second. The soft spoken, quiet professional, backbone of the Corporation's program who happily accepts the supporting role, behind Commander Madison Glen.

She would be the face of the Program, chosen by the Corporation to be the standard bearer for the next great human achievement. Human light-speed travel -- The Leap. And for that flight, Thomas Harry Jenson is the backup, standing ready should anything go wrong. Should everything go well, he is ready, still. Ready to be second.

Thomas Harry Jenson is destined to be the Gus Grissom of his generation, and that means he is destined to be the forgotten one. No one remembers the second. Gus Grissom came after Alan Shepard, and who remembers Gus Grissom? Who was the second pilot across the Atlantic, *after* Lindbergh?

But Thomas Harry Jenson doesn't care about the answer. It is not in his blood to care about such things. He does not crave glory. He believes in the science and in the mission. He is, after all, the son of T.H. Jenson Sr., the first great theorist of manned light travel. A believer in its possibilities, and a furious inquisitor of its effects on the mind. A divisive figure within the rarified world of trans-light biophysics. They still talk about his theories today, sixty years after his disappearance. And, for now, they still argue.

You think you know of Thomas Harry Jenson's brief and unhappy marriage. Even the Corporation cannot hide this, though it can shape the narrative. The dedicated wife, herself a leading physician-researcher of neuroplasticity and cerebral trauma. The husband and wife, torn apart by their discreet professional passions. Their only mutual success, a child, a boy, by all accounts a genius in his own right. You think you know these stories, or if you did once, you have forgotten them. That's fine. These characters are sideshows. His father does not matter. His marriage and his son are unknown to most of you. There is only Thomas Harry Jenson.

The man understands his role. He understands that Commander Glen must be the first and he is accepting of that. He sees that she is the equal of every pilot in the Corporation and has mastered every procedure Thomas Harry Jenson has developed. She has honed every skill the mission demands. When she is not in the cockpit, the laboratory, the classroom, the mess, she is saying the perfect things to the people, the media and the multi-eyed monster of video-world. She is the Earhart of Lightspeed.

But you all know what happens then. How Commander Glen returns from her first near-light training mission. The longest journey yet and the first outside a simulator. Two months in duration. One month's passage through the Newtonian Belt to our solar system's perimeter, to the edge of the Einstein Expanse. There, a day of preparation, locking in the optimal vector for unobstructed acceleration to Sub-Light Injection. It is the final test before the Super Light Transit and it goes off without a hitch.

Commander Madison Glen travels closer to light speed than any human ever, a speed she maintains for less than three seconds, more than twice the time she will spend at light speed, on the follow-up mission – the main event – two months later.

Commander Glen returns from her mission already a hero. You know this part. You watched live or have seen the footage on History Network. The ratings. The hits. The likes. Only the Corporation's frantic schedule limits the amount of press she can do. A visit to the White House is postponed only because Commander Glen must get back to work. She buries herself once again into the Program. This is well documented. The Corporation has deadlines. The next best window for launch into The Expanse approaches and the Program cannot wait.

When Commander Glen disappears the Corporation launches a search and the Program continues with Thomas Harry Jenson in the seat. The search does not take long. Commander Glen's body is found deep in a ravine spanned by a highway bridge three hundred meters above. Her head is opened on rocks, the result of rapid deceleration after falling at high speed from a great height for a fleeting time.

This sounds strange to you, I know. You don't know this part because no one has told you. The Corporation has not released the truth, because it has decided the Program could not withstand the publicity. This is what you have been told instead: that Commander Glen died in a single vehicle accident. You saw the images of the crash. You heard the eulogies. You read the tributes.

You know that Thomas Harry Jenson became the new number one pilot, and everyone thinks they know what happened next. How could you not? Before it is over, everyone on earth knows his name.

But none of you really knows the story. You still don't. Because it's not over.

2

The Flight Surgeon asks, How have you been since the Commander's death?

Thomas Harry Jenson says, I'm fine, Flight. Really. He calls his doctor Flight. It's what all the pilots in the Program call the doctor.

Flight says, What about her death. How are you feeling about that?

It was sad.

Can you elaborate?

It was sad when she died.

Is that all?

It presented difficult challenges for the Program, but everything has returned to nominal status.

You're on schedule?

We're on schedule.

You don't strike me as sad. You don't look sad?

What does that look like?

Back to your schedule. Are you concerned about its additional demands?

Demands?

You were scheduled to fly in four months. That's been cut to two. Not a lot of time.

There's enough.

There will be no time for a test run to the Sub-Light Injection point that Commander Glen experienced. You'll only have the one flight.

The solution at two months has a superior margin. It's a logical choice for a first attempt at the transit. There's little to be gained by waiting. And our simulators are superb.

Are simulators enough?

They will have to be.

How does all this make you feel?

I'm fine, Flight. I really am.

* * *

HIS SON WAITS OUTSIDE THE DOCTOR'S OFFICE. HE IS FIFTEEN, IN HIS second year of university and has taken the day off to spend it with his father. He can afford the time. He's top of his class in both majors, astrodynamics and artificial intelligence systems. He spends his class time mastering the worlds of Newton, Einstein, Turing and their many descendants. In his spare time he corrects text books. As they leave the medical centre, Thomas Harry Jenson recounts his conversation with Flight and his son asks him if he thinks two months really is enough time.

I designed the systems.

His son knows this, so that's not an answer. He doubts one is forthcoming, so he changes the subject.

I've been reading about the Apollo missions, and about Mars One.

In your spare time.

The adaptation curve between flights was notoriously difficult for the early astronauts.

They didn't design the systems they were operating.

It wasn't the systems. It was the physical experiences of prolonged flight that forced the curve.

We've been traveling in space for a long time now. What kind of experiences?

I know. I've also read about the Io and Europa missions, and the medical logs of Exo-planet crews. There's a lot about the physical stresses.

We know about those.

But also mental. Psychological.

Thomas Harry Jenson thinks about this, and his son can't help feeling pleased. He has caused the machine to pause.

Then the Commander says, Such as?

There were differing descriptions. Many described anxiety.

That wouldn't be surprising.

There were other symptoms. Mood swings. Euphoria then sudden depression.

We know more now.

A few used a strange word to describe their feelings. Displacement.

Displacement? What does that even mean?

They reach the car and the father instructs it to take them to the boy's campus residence.

Getting in the vehicle his son says, Do we know more yet about what happened to Commander Glen?

I don't.

There are rumours that it wasn't a car accident. The Corporation is covering something up.

Like what?

There was something wrong with her.

Wrong?

The son can't decide if he will persist because he is sure he will get nothing from the effort. Then he remembers.

Why are you taking me to res?

It's where you live. You have studying to do.

You promised mom.

It's bad timing.

The hospice is expecting us. And you promised mom.

Today isn't good.

Mom said that's what you'd say.

Did she tell you what to say when I said that?

Yes.

And?

To tell you that I want to go and you promised me too.

Anything else?

That Granpa will be disappointed.

Granpa won't know.

Mom says he will. She says he's still Granpa on the inside. And you did promise.

They sit silently for a few more seconds, the vehicle humming past a landscape of thousand-year old Joshua trees and billion-year old golden sand.

His father says to the car at last, Reroute. To grandfather's.

The car listens. It has plotted a new course before Thomas Harry Jenson has finished saying grand.

3

THEY ARE SCANNED THROUGH THE HIGH-SECURITY LOBBY OF THE Corporation's hospice and shown to Granpa's location by a personal service bot. This quality of care is a benefit afforded by the Corporation for the legendary father of the legendary pilot. They find Granpa in the large common area, sitting alone. The boy kneels, looks at the old man and takes stock. His eyes are wet and locked on something on the other side of the recreation room. Or locked on nothing. The boy thinks what he always thinks: *What do you see, Granpa? What are you thinking? What do you feel?*

Thomas Harry Jenson stands on the other side of the room looking at them both. The boy sees him thinking: *Let's get this over with.*

The boy kneels there, for a moment feeling sandwiched between generations. He stares at his grandparent, and says to his father, When's the last time you were here?

I've been busy, his father answers.

I'm just asking.

A while.

When was the last time you talked to him?

I don't know. A long time.

What did you talk about?

His work. His theories.

About light speed and time?

And other things.

What other things.

Thomas Harry Jenson doesn't answer. Maybe because he doesn't remember or maybe because he does. Maybe he thinks it doesn't matter because why would it matter when your father hasn't said your name in two years.

They sit like that for a time.

The boy asks, How old were you when Granpa developed his theories on light travel and the mind?

I only learned about it when I was in university, when they taught it to me.

He didn't tell you himself?

No.

Neither did Gramma?

She had left a long time before. I didn't see her much. But she never told me. And I didn't see much of him either. So I didn't know.

The boy thinks about this.

At university, did they know who your father was?

Eventually.

So you had a famous father too when you were in school.

I'm not famous.

You're famous enough. And you'll be more famous soon, says the boy. Then he looks back to his grandfather and an idea occurs.

You should tell him what's happening.

It's a waste. He can't process it. He may not even be able to hear.

Mom thinks he hears. You should tell him.

You tell him yourself if you want, Thomas Harry Jenson says, looking at his watch.

So the boy does it for him. He tells his grandfather about the mission his father will perform, leaving out the story of Commander Glen, only talking about what is present and now, or what is about to happen. Thomas Harry Jenson barely listens. He looks out the window, across the plain toward where the sun will set, and he thinks about the better ways he could have spent this day. About its cost in time and the waste of it. But something stops him, makes him look back at the two of them. His son has finished his story and now he is leaning in toward his grandfather, his ear turned to the old man's mouth. He doesn't pull back, not until the old man's lips stop moving, then the boy stands up, stretched to his full height, and looks to his father who asks the question.

What did he say?

The boy repeats his grandfather's words.

Bring me with you.

4

THE NEXT PART YOU KNOW. YOU MUST. IT IS HISTORY. LIKE MAGELLAN. Like Yeager and Gagarin and Armstrong. Commander Thomas Harry Jenson passes through the Newtonian Belt, the planetary zone of our solar system where Sir Isaac's laws of action and reaction dominate. After this he prepares for the SLT phase, where he will escape Newtonian laws and enter Einstein's realm. Where time changes.

And history is made. The mission is a success. The achievement is checked and double checked, verified by an international board of the best minds in their field, representing more than a dozen countries and at least three competitor companies. Even the competition must yield to the facts. Light speed has been maintained. For just one point nine-three seconds, craft and man together travel the speed of light, a length of time sufficient to prove the possibility, but brief enough to minimize relativity's effects. If time has frozen for Thomas Harry Jenson, it has done so with little or no effect.

The Leap is a success and the pilot has returned to earth. To all appearances healthy and unchanged by his experience.

* * *

THERE WERE HONOURS AND PARADES AND SPEECHES AND DIGNITARIES and awards. There were remembrances of the brave Commander Glen, who paved the way. It is all that you would expect and everything you might imagine. But you don't have to imagine, because you know all this. It's part of the story and it's all mostly true.

But there are some other things you do not know. Such as how much Thomas Harry Jenson hated the being-famous time.

How all he wanted was to go back to work.

That he was finding it harder and harder to sleep.

That he couldn't remember anything that happened around the time of light speed transit.

And the tremors. You haven't heard about those.

All of this was part of the story too, only there's no way you could know that.

5

THIS IS HOW A TREMOR BEGINS. WHAT COMES FIRST IS THE AURA. NOT a glow like he has heard from those who endure migraines. Not a scent either. It is a sound. A deep humming tone that comes from somewhere inside his ear, like tinnitus only not. This is a *basso* rumble, low and rich and building, at once electronic *and* organic.

He cannot ignore the hum. Because it is a prelude to the tremor.

It happens to anything living and moving around him. A dog or a cat. A coyote loping through a gully. Even people. Especially people. The tremor is the sense that any moving thing is vibrating from somewhere deep inside. Like it has swallowed something powerful, something that is spinning and pushing the object, its host, forward at the same time. Bodies moving, somehow simultaneously robotic and fluid. Like an old-style film put suddenly on fast-forward for a short burst, then back to normal speed. In the first occurrences, the bursts are very short. Look up from a menu at a dining room to see the guests and waiters spasming into furious action. Then an eyeblink. Then back to normal.

Thomas Harry Jenson tries to dismiss the first auras. The sound builds, but not to painful levels, then the short burst of the tremor happens - in a restaurant, on the walk to his office, at lunch in the mess – but so brief, such a burst of hyper energetic motion – it's as if it never happens. Something he can barely remember.

Even as they grow in frequency, he is able to suppress them. He takes a breath, finds his center. Refocuses his thoughts. Returns his mind to the job at hand.

But it is not always so easy. The tremors grow. In length. In intensity.

The first aura, followed by the first tremor event, happens one week after his return. There were two that day. The next day there were six. Then down to five. Then seven. Then ten. Always short and random bursts accompanying the deep, humming tone, sharp and thick and ancient.

But as they grow – as they become *deeper* – the aura and the tremor together are joined by something else he cannot recognize. Not at first. This may be because it is something that doesn't come naturally to him. It is a feeling.

* * *

HE IS IN THE MEDICAL CENTRE, TWO WEEKS AFTER THE COMPLETION OF his mission. He sits on the edge of an examining table, waiting to give yet another blood sample for yet another test. The Tech is programming the equipment, telling the cyber nursing unit which arm and how much blood to draw.

Which is when the deep thrumming sound begins. Thomas Harry Jenson feels it coming. This is the twelfth event of the day. The last was less than an hour before. That had not been what he would call a full-scale tremor. More of an aftershock or perhaps a prelude. He hopes this will be the same. He prepares.

It isn't the same. The hum is now a full-body pulse, gripping his being and forcing his eyes shut until he opens them and the medical technician is jetting across his field of vision and the door to the observation room wings open and another technician buzzes into the room and the two speak to each other at a speed that renders language into a high insectoid hissing. This event is lasting. It's going on. It isn't ending. He closes his eyes to make it go away and when he opens them – it's still going on. The rattling fast, staccato movements. The technician leaves the conversation with his colleague and walks to the cyber nurse, gives final high-pitched instructions, turns away as the machine approaches the examining table. All of that happens in a fraction of a second, accompanied by the horrible, thick humming noise. And now it all comes with something else.

Terror. Fury. Two things Thomas Harry Jenson has never felt and two things that now conspire, by-passing the thinking part of his mind and cinching themselves into his amygdala, the home of his reptile brain, his survival instinct, the place where we keep the claws and fangs.

So there is no thought that comes to him. Only action. He lashes out. Somehow before the hyperactive medical machine with its gyrating mechanical arms can get too close, he leans away from it. He braces himself on the table with his hands on its edge, raises a foot to the oncoming face of the machine and kicks with all he has.

And as fast as that, the event is over. The act breaks the spell. Or the worst of it. Everything around him has stopped. The two technicians are staring dumbly at him, then down at the bot lying in pieces, its articulated arms splayed across the tiles.

Thomas Harry Jenson stares back. Sees what he has done. Sees the technicians. He gets off the table and walks out the door.

Something else happens while he walks. Motion provides relief. The thrumming, distant now, begins fading faster. The remaining fear and anger dissipate. With a few tentative strides he begins to trot, then to jog. Down the hall, to a stairwell, which he takes two steps at a time, then out the door of the medical centre.

With every stride he feels better. He flies on his feet.

6

FLIGHT SAYS, THANKS FOR COMING IN COMMANDER. WE NEED TO talk.

I'm sorry about the damage, says Thomas Harry Jenson.

You gave our boys a bit of a fright, but they'll recover. Can you tell me what happened?

He explains as best as he can, describing the symptoms, their frequency, the growing intensity.

How have your nights been? Do you sleep?

Not very well. Last night I got a good couple of hours, then woke.

What woke you?

I think it was the noise. It's like a very deep string on a giant viola or cello somewhere in my head. Anyway, I woke up and decided I wasn't going to just lie there and wait for the event to happen.

What did you do?

I drove. I got in my vehicle and just took the desert road.

And then what?

I just drove. It helped.

How?

I don't know how, but the sound faded. I ... I calmed down and I was able to get back home after a while and get some sleep. The episode that I thought was coming never came.

Just like that?

There's something else I've noticed. It seemed to get better the faster I went. Relief from the sound, and the anxiety. Once I was able to get the vehicle out into the barrens and really open it up, I just felt ... fine. Or nearly.

Flight took notes on a tablet.

How long ago was that, when did you come back from your drive?

About four hours now.

And how do you feel? Now?

I don't know. I'm not sure.

Is the sound happening? Are you getting the aura?

No. But I will.

You sound sure.

I am.

I need to observe you. When you're having an episode.

When do you want to do this?

Now. I want to keep you here. We'll watch.

I think that will be a mistake.

Why? How else can I help you?

I just don't think…I'm not ready.

Look, Commander Jenson. The Corporation has given me clear direction. You destroyed an awfully expensive piece of equipment yesterday and, frankly, you are a very valuable company asset as well. We're all concerned, Commander.

Yes, but you don't understand, I can't stay here and be watched.

While Thomas Harry Jenson speaks, Flight removes a small dermapatch from his lab coat pocket. His patient doesn't notice, and continues talking, explaining his fear.

If you want to be where you can observe me, then you have to be ready to follow me, because when the episode happens…I'll have to move and move fast…It's all I can think of to do.

But when he says"move" the second time he feels the flight surgeon's hand press firmly on the back of his own right hand, and pulling away, sees the patch.

What's this?

A sedative.

Thomas Harry Jenson tries to peel the patch away from his skin, but he is already feeling its effects.

Stop it. Take it off me. You can't do this…

But the patch has done its work, and Thomas Harry Jenson says his final words before passing out.

I can hear the sound. It's coming…

And then all goes black.

* * *

WHEN HE REGAINS CONSCIOUSNESS, THE FACE OF HIS FLIGHT SURGEON is above his own, looking down on him.

Thomas Harry Jenson says, How long have I been out?

What do you remember?

Nothing.

How do you feel?

He lifts his arms, attempts to sit. Cannot. Realizes two things. He is sore in every joint. And he is restrained, at the wrists and ankles and across the chest. He pulls again and it hurts again.

You have to let me move.

What are you feeling now?

Unstrap me.

Listen, Flight says. Can you hear that?

There's a steady sequence of electronic beeps, pinging at an impossible speed.

Look at the screen, Flight says.

With effort he tilts his head upward and sees a dark blue screen, a bright blur of a white line is carving up and down across the monitor's width, pinging up and down, up and down.

That's your heart rate.

That's impossible.

I know. Five-hundred beats per minute. You should be dead according to that line.

Then Flight says, Don't move.

He puts two fingers on his patient's carotid artery. His hand is cool. He looks at his watch for ten seconds.

Flight says, It's the same every time and it doesn't make sense. I have you at ninety per minute. Tops.

The machine is wrong.

I've had you connected to three different monitors. All say the same. Obviously it can't be your heart rate they're reading, but it's reading something that's happening to you...

Why am I tied down?

...something that none of us can see.

Why the straps?

You've been seizing. After the sedative kicked in you were calm for about a minute, and then you...

Flight can't find the word. Then it comes.

You exploded. Every limb in a different direction. You were like a top, almost spinning on the table, going nowhere, like there was something inside of you, forcing you to move. It took five of us to control you.

That is when Thomas Harry Jenson hears the first distant *thrumming* ... the low, distant bass that he tries to ignore. He mustn't show anything.

He says to his doctor, Flight, look, can you let me stretch out a bit here? I think the worst has passed.

Thrumm...thruuummm...it's building.

Yes, I suppose, says Flight. It seems pretty clear sedation isn't the way to go.

He starts on an ankle strap. At the same time an orderly comes in the room, a sturdy and wary young man. Perhaps one of the team that just finished battling with his spasming body.

The sound is building...but not so fast...not so fast that he can feel it yet. There may be time.

Flight instructs the orderly to continue removing the restraints and looks back at Thomas Harry Jenson, studying him. Then says, There's something else.

Thrummm...thruuuum... please hurry.

Flight is holding something ... a mirror.

Thomas Harry Jenson looks at himself. It's not dramatic, but there is no mistaking the change. There are crow's feet at his eyes, there is a fine white stubble on his chin, and grey peppers the hair at his temples.

Flight says, I can't say for sure when it happened. I only noticed after we had you back under control.

Is it five years of age? Is it ten? It's impossible to say. It's also almost impossible to think because the sound has now truly arrived and overtaken him.

Thruuuummmm....THRUMMMMMMMM...MMMMMMMM. It's a groaning animal at the base of his skull. Words are beyond him.

Flight misreads his patient's expression, takes it for confusion, and continues to explain.

You were out for only ten minutes. We brought you back as soon as we could, in case the sedation had an aggravating effect on your condition.

Flight's patient is now free of restraints. The last words that Thomas Harry Jenson hears that register in his untethered mind are *aggregating effect*, and, in a state of mind beyond the appreciation of irony, the patient flashes the heel of an open palm in a vicious piston motion directly under the chin of the Flight Surgeon, throwing the doctor backwards stumbling against a wall of equipment before his legs lose their composure and crumple beneath him. As the doctor falls, Thomas Harry Jenson is half-way to the door of the observation room when the orderly is on him. The orderly is a bigger, quicker man, and much younger.

But not too big, and not that quick, and age is no matter, because now the Thrumming has taken over. He can feel it in every move and step and twitch of muscle. He looks at the younger man and without knowing how it has happened, the orderly is on the floor holding a useless arm against his chest as he writhes on the cold tiles.

What happens next he only remembers later, piecing it together when there is time. When he can review the events.

Running from the medical centre he finds a vehicle belonging to the Corporation. Its passwords and speed governor are both easily defeated. He drives, pushing his limits and the vehicle's.

He doesn't know how long he must drive and he has no need for direction other than to find the straightest path possible.

The longest and the straightest. That is where real speed can happen.

7

You DO NOT KNOW THIS. ONLY I KNOW THIS PART. AND THE Corporation, of course.

The stolen car, taken from the Corporation lot on the night of Commander Thomas Harry Jenson's initial disappearance, is found near that stretch of highway that spans the great ravine, the same bridge from which Commander Madison Glen was presumed to have leapt to her death only three months before. The vehicle is a shattered, burned out hulk when

Corporate police find it. Work is commenced immediately to confirm whether or not there were any occupants. Calculations show that the vehicle was travelling at a tremendous speed at the moment of impact.

* * *

THE SON OF THOMAS HARRY JENSON TAKES A CALL FROM THE FLIGHT Surgeon, in which the doctor conveys terrible news: it appears Commander Jenson has died in a high-speed, single-vehicle accident, similar to the kind of accident that killed Commander Glen. A tragic and freak coincidence. It has not been confirmed as yet and an investigation is still underway. The media, of course, have not been informed. The surgeon offers condolences and signs off.

Before he can begin to properly grieve, the son is extremely surprised and relieved to hear the buzzer at the front door to his apartment and to see his father standing there.

Over the course of that evening the father explains to the son what has happened. After driving the stolen vehicle at maximum speed for more than an hour, he had found - if not normalcy - a condition of equilibrium at least. He could think at last, the speed of the car gave him that much.

The speed? The boy asks, interrupting.

It's only a theory. It's all that makes sense. With every episode that I experience, I have two choices. I can try to ride it out, or I can find some way to fend it off.

Fend it off?

Or just delay it, I don't know which. At first, when the events began, I found that just sprinting down a hallway could bring me relief. I thought it might be adrenaline or even simple dopamine that my body was craving.

But you don't think that anymore.

No. Early on, maybe it helped. In the clinic, two weeks ago, when I had a violent reaction and kicked that cyber unit, it helped, but it was a temporary. The only thing that really brought me back was actual physical motion.

The car you stole. Your Flight Surgeon said it was traveling beyond twice it's limiter's ability.

Almost three times. The feeling was...

The boy watches his father trying to describe a feeling, something he has never seen or heard him do. And his father's face, older than he remembers it (even from just a week before) but now somehow rejuvenated at the memory of the car's high-speed transit of the great desert...

Glorious, says his father, finally finding the word and shaking his head.

You would have been proud of my system hack, Thomas Harry Jenson continues. Though I'm sure you could have done it in less time than I took.

Did you also hack the crash?

Yes. I want the Corporation to think I'm dead. At least for a little while. I need to buy some time.

How much time?

A week. Maybe two. I'll need to stay with you.

It is not an unreasonable request, but still the son says no.

I have a better idea, says the boy.

8

THE ASSUMPTION IS THAT THERE WILL BE SURVEILLANCE. THE SON arranges for Thomas Harry Jenson to stay at a fellow student's apartment in an adjacent residence block (the regular tenant being on a work term, observing blue whales off the Baja coast). Communications between the two of them will be offline, through black market devices, still the best way to guarantee discretion.

They agree it is best if face to face contact is kept to a minimum. The father will relay his daily experiences as best he can, so the son can keep records, provide a backup resource as chronicler of Thomas Harry Jenson's progress. Or his failure.

* * *

Day 1: Inbound message: San Andreas bullet train to the Bay Area and back. The longest, high-speed journey I've taken to date. Symptoms abated for its duration. Relief is short-lived though. Perhaps because the speed provides no euphoria, perhaps due to its consistency or the fact it never approaches the peak speeds attained in the desert car rides. My first hint of aura happened four hours after pulling into the station.

Day 2: Inbound message: Found a parasailing outfit run out of San Jose. Though distracting and thrilling, the speeds attained, outside of the steepest dives (which are unsustainable for any significant amount of time), and the overall duration of the entire flight is inadequate to have any enduring remedial impact. The view is nice. But my state of mind gives little space to enjoy it.

Day 3: Inbound message: Base jumping. Expensive, but fantastic in its short-term impact. It has a quick fix quality that I will keep in mind. The fact is that maximum velocity doesn't match either train or a doctored car. Perhaps it is the fact of being uncontained in a vehicle that the effect is so dramatic.

Day 4: Inbound message: Did five jumps today. That is seven over the course of the last two days. I have had to ingratiate myself to the tower manager with some money and - shocking for me - charm. Let's call it charm anyway, though that is something no one ever accused me of having before this "condition" of mine.

(Is that a happy side-effect of this war my mind is waging?)

On my final jump of the day, in a moment that I can only think of as a clarifying experience, I was in the last seconds before pulling my chute when a thought occurred to me. The height of the ravine bridge back at the desert is almost as high a base tower jump. If Commander Madison's death was a suicide, and if she had suffered the same or similar condition, it's likely that the desperation and trauma she felt standing there, before jumping, would have vanished some time just before she hit the floor of the desert. Maybe as she made impact.

If that's the case - and it appears to be - then how cruel it is that the only cure for this condition that I have found is, ultimately, fatal.

But only if taken in excessive doses I suppose.

Listen to me. That almost sounds like I made a joke. Another first for your old dad.

(Maybe the side-effects are worth it?)

You're forgiven for not laughing.

Day 6: Inbound message: Using base jumping as a "fix" that enables me to keep my cognitive and processing skills intact, I have taken a chance and moved on a plan. I have reached out to a contact at the Corporation and tried to arrange an afternoon in one of the Corporation's experimental solarwing high-altitude aircraft. Nothing more than jet propelled but put into a dive it could deliver a speed dose of considerable effect. Also, the solarwing can stay aloft for prolonged periods. This may not be a solution, but it will be a big fix. (Pardon the drug addict pun, but they're becoming hard to avoid.)

While I wait to hear back from my associate, I have scheduled a visit to a local bungee jumping concern south of town. The base jumps are too expensive to be sustainable, and I'm running the risk of becoming a local celebrity. Attention I don't need.

Day 6: Outbound message: Careful who you trust. I'll remain watchful.

Day 7: Inbound message: Bungee jumping, cheaper than base jumping, and more or less equivalent in its impact. Good news. The bad news, however, is that I feel a diminution over time of the remediating effect of each jump, or even a series of jumps. I truly am like any drug addict, experiencing an increasing immunity to counter-medications, building up tolerances with every dose. Is that my ultimate curse? Is it possible that the only antidote to not enough speed ... is more speed? If that's true, then what hope do I have?

Still waiting for my chance to fly the solarwing. I won't lie, the waiting is hard. But I will remain patient and wait for my contact to reach back.

Day 7: Outbound message: All clear on my end. No sign of surveillance. By the way: I'm rereading Granpa's notes in the stacks at school. When the first trains were invented, back in the eighteen-hundreds, they were the fastest vehicles on earth. Scientists of the day doubted the human body would cope with speeds of fifty miles-an-hour. They were wrong, of course, but Granpa cites their influence on his thinking. He says it's where he began. It started his exploration of the effects of time and speed on the mind and body. He just asked - what if? We should discuss his theories. There may be application. No cures that I can see, yet. I'm sorry. Only insights. But maybe that will help.

Day 10: Inbound message: Last two days have been hard. The Bungee jumping is having less impact. So... I'm afraid I did something stupid. The lad who runs the bungee tower mentioned a friend who operates a wingsuit studio. You've seen them in videos. The pilot, who is really no more than a projectile, is zipped into a large one-piece coverall that is designed to create a human-sized square wing configuration when the wearer holds their arms and legs out in a starfish shape. The resemblance is of a flying squirrel. You put on the suit and jump off a cliff. If it's high enough you could have a flight that's close to ten minutes and speeds near terminal velocity. They give you a helmet as well, but that's superfluous. If something goes wrong, there's not much help in headgear.

I'm only telling you this because it will be useful for the record. It will speak to the extremity of my addiction. (Let's call it what it is, shall we.)

I lied to the wingsuit person about the experience and any other prerequisites required and paid the last of the cash I have. I will tell you only that I survived.

I won't try that again.

The good news is, it worked. I will sleep tonight. The bad news is, if the day comes that I find myself in that state again, I believe I will make a trip to the bridge over Commander Glen's ravine.

I am tired. I am ... what's the word you used that time, the word you read from the early astronauts? I am feeling ... displacement.

And I am running out of options.

Day 10: Inbound supplemental: My contact at the Corporation has reached me. He says the plane is ready. Finally. Tomorrow.

Day 10: Outbound: Important dad. I can't be sure, but I think I'm seeing a strange vehicle in the student compound. It may be surveillance. Be careful. Can you trust your contact? All Corporation planes have transponders for tracking. Make sure it's disabled. Also, I may have found something in Granpa's theories. In a chapter on relativity's impact on organic life. We know Granpa believed humans could make the leap, but this chapter adds to that. It theorizes the possibility that light travel could make changes to human physiology. We know about its impact on material, mechanical things. You accounted for that in the design of the ship. But we couldn't redesign the brain before departure. What does that mean for the human mind at light speed?

Is it possible that one point nine three seconds at the speed of light has rewired your brain? Is it possible you can't unwire it?

I'm scared. This is beyond my abilities dad. Even beyond yours. We need help. Let me ask at the research institute. I have a supervisor I believe I can trust. Just say the word. Please.

Day 13: Inbound message: Son, the solarwing has worked wonders. Don't worry, if I am being surveilled there are no signs. I was able to do a half day of high-speed maneuvers and the feeling, for now, is satisfactory. For the first time in days, I feel a clarity I can't remember having any time since returning from the mission. But I now know it's only temporary. I also know you are right. We need more information. With the help of my Corporation contact, I arranged a meeting with Flight. You remember that my last visit with him didn't end on the most trusting terms, but credit where it's due, he understood. He told me everything he knows, at least I think it's everything.

It isn't very good news.

The Corporation has suspected the threat to cerebral function since early in the Program's development. They knew all about the literature, including your Granpa's theory. No mission pilots were told, of course. Why tell the people with the most to lose? The theory only became fact when they did the autopsy on Commander Glen. They still don't know what they were looking at when they saw her brain tissue, only that it was different. Unlike anything they had seen. But they knew the difference was caused by the near-light experience. That was the only explanation. Somehow her mind developed this appetite for speed that she could not feed. In one week, she went from clinical genius to voracious addict. And then she threw herself off a bridge. Flight doesn't know why near-light affected her so severely, while I seem to have been able to resist. Flight thinks I may have built up a resistance, by not being cooped up in simulators the way she was in her prolonged prep period of almost two years. While she sat stationary in a virtual experience machine, I flew real cockpit hours. Cross-country, intercontinental. We know that even terrestrial sub-Mach travel has infinitesimal effects on material substances. Maybe hits of speed act as micro-doses to the mind too. A time vaccine. Prior to my flight, the tight schedule gave me only two months in the simulator. Two months of sitting perfectly still, pretending to travel at light speed, but going nowhere. But just two months. Maybe that's what has bought me this time.

Whatever the case, as hard as it is to say to you, I now know I'm a lucky man. I may be slowly going insane, and I may be running out of ways to buy more time, but at least I've had this chance to understand what has happened to me.

Even if I can't stop it, there's dignity in knowing what they have done to me. And knowing I have you as a son. There is that too.

9

A LONG TIME PASSES AFTER THAT LAST MESSAGE. AN AMOUNT OF TIME that, to the son, feels dilated and contorted. His father has gone silent. The vehicles that have hovered in the student plaza have gone away, and a day later, the Corporation re-releases the images, from three weeks before, of the crash scene. He sees again the twisted and scorched metal of the vehicle his father programmed to crash. He hears the somber voice-over announcing confirmation of the tragic death of Thomas Harry Jenson. A hero dies. The world mourns. A nation weeps.

The Corporation reorganizes. The son hears no word from the Flight Surgeon. This time the Flight Director calls, extending heartfelt apologies and ending her message with an odd coda.

She says - If there is anything about your father you would like to report, please don't hesitate. Have a good day.

The son wonders.

What is there to report about a dead man?

10

Day 33: Inbound message: Son, I am sorry to have run silent for so long. I am sorry for the pain this has caused.

You were right to not trust the Corporation. The day after meeting Flight, I returned to the solarwing for another half-day of self-medicating. (It is a glorious thing living near a desert, as we do. Millions of miles of flat nothing to hide in.) I took it to altitude and was about to pitch into my first dive when I saw the drones. Two tactical, utility craft, small and agile, designed to scare wildlife and inspect runways mostly, but programmable for most anything the Corporation requires of them.

Both of them were also heavily armed.

But I'm a good pilot. I welcomed the challenge and, obvious by my presence now, was able to evade them both. (And get a fairly remarkable hit of speed for my troubles; thank you very much, Flight.)

Maybe that last dose was the key, or the clarity of being betrayed in the ways that I have, but the plan came to me quite quickly after that.

So, I need your help again. Once you have read this, delete the message and destroy your device. You know what you're doing. I know this. I think there may be a way out of this mess that can still end in both of us staying alive.

You are the only one I can trust now, son. You and one other.

I'll see you in two days.

Read on.

11

IT MAY SURPRISE YOU TO HEAR THIS, BUT IT'S TRUE. FOR PILOT, programmer, designer, Thomas Harry Jenson, stealing a light-speed test craft is a simple matter. Flying it when the time comes will be an equally simple matter. The ship is the one he trained on while he was the second in line on the mission's rolls.

His son's job is to smuggle his grandfather out of the Corporation's AI-managed, high security hospice. This is a simple hack for a very bright young man. The next job is to get his grandfather to the Corporation's launch headquarters. All things considered, the son does not find his talents stretched.

In the midst of his smuggling efforts, with his arm around his grandfather, it dawns with great clarity what Thomas Harry Jenson meant in his last message to his son, when he said - I think there is a way out of this mess that can still end with both of us staying alive.

Both of us - the son understands - does not include the son. He will stay behind. That makes sense. His life, his mind, is not in jeopardy. His clock is not ticking so loudly.

It is possible they may never be able to return to earth. A million things can go wrong. How long they can stay at light speed is one variable; how much time passes on earth while they are at light speed is a calculation Thomas Harry Jenson is uncertain of. Einstein only asked the question. He never answered it.

What happens to them at light speed - how their minds will change, rewire, unwire, improve, diminish - all of that is unknown as well.

All that is certain is what happens if they remain on Earth. That alternative, he has decided, is no alternative at all.

* * *

TWO MONTHS AFTER LAUNCH, TO THE DAY, THE SON RETRIEVES FROM beneath a loose floorboard in his residence room a small device his father gave him on the Corporation launch pad.

His instructions, given that launch day, are simple and clear.

On the launch pad, his father tells him the comms system will be activated only once he has finalized the trajectory for launch into the Expanse. The signal the son hears will be the same that is received by the Corporation's Mission Office. It may be traceable, so the son is to activate the receiver only in time for the Transit point. That is the only time his father will activate ship-to-earth comms, so that is the only way to know if they have made it that far.

There has been no publicity around the theft of the Corporation's spacecraft. Not surprising perhaps, as its thief is a man the Corporation has pronounced dead. The boy draws no joy from the thought from the Corporation's embarrassment; it is, after all, very likely that his father is in fact dead already, and his grandfather with him.

The son sits at his desk where he has placed the small receiver and, at the instructed time, turns it on. A single red pinhead of light glows to signal activation. He listens. He doesn't have to wait long for the static, then a voice.

Not his father. It is a voice of the Corporation.

This is Mission Office. We are reading your signal. Do you read us, Commander, over?

The son knows he has time. It will take almost five hours for the Mission Office message to reach the edge of the solar system. Another five for the response.

He's waited this long. He'll wait some more.

When the next voice comes, once again it is not the voice of his father.

Hello Mission Office. This is Thomas Harry Jenson, Senior. We are preparing for Super Light Transit. See you on the other side.

It might be the son's imagination, but in that miniscule moment between the voice of his grandfather signing off and the final click of silence he is sure he hears his father.

A sound of laughter coming from the edge of deep space.

12

THERE HAVE BEEN REPORTS CIRCULATING THROUGH THE DEPARTMENT at the polytechnic where I still teach. A younger colleague has reached out to his contacts and confirmed them for me. A small spacecraft, possibly capable of light speed, has been detected reentering our solar system. It has the navigation beacon consistent with the old Corporation crafts of nearly fifty years ago. There are also reports that perimeter scanners have picked up readings of two healthy humans.

Tugs are being sent, complete with emergency medical and technical crews, to make sure the small craft finishes its final leg.

I wish I could join those tugs, so I could improve my chances of greeting the crew, but for now it is enough to know that it is the perimeter scanning system I have designed that has been able to pick them up, and alert our planet of the return of earth's two greatest travelers of time and space. It's a good feeling to know I played a hand in their recovery. At least I did not waste the time I was given. I did not want to let them down.

The Corporation is long gone now. I doubt anyone will even remember its name. The Flight Surgeon, is gone too, though I feel some regret in this. I would like him to have witnessed this moment, the safe return to earth of the man he betrayed. But no one lives that long.

No one, that is, except for those who travel at the speed of light.

There should be no serious obstacle now to finally telling you all the truth of the story. What really happened to Thomas Harry Jenson. And to his father, my grandfather.

Though, until they are here with me, until I can put an arm around each of them, there still is some dread I feel. I ask myself once more, could I join one of the tugs, as some kind of honorary observer? But no. No, there are rules, and I broke enough of them before I was old enough to fly. No, I will have to wait. Even if I am the genius son of a genius son of a genius father.

There is nothing more to do now, but to wait. Even if the time is killing me.

Because what I do not know is what is happening inside that faraway craft. What I do know is that it is no longer traveling at the speed of light. It has left the realm of Einstein and relativity. The time they are living in now, once again, is my time. Your time. And time is leaking away.

The ship with its voyagers is entering the competing gravitational fields of our solar system, and then, inevitably the pull of Earth and its dense, buffeting atmosphere.

They are coming home, and with every passing moment...slowing down, joining us, here where we are all the children of Newton's laws. Where we all must slow down.

When that happens, when they open the hatch and look inside, there may be poetry or there may be horror.

When that happens, we will all know how the story ends.

Vintage Venus

By Nick Forster

WAR RAGED ACROSS THE GALAXY, BUT SOME STILL SOUGHT PEACE, searching out finer things in life, music, literature, wine. So it was that Captain Gort spent his days, a merchant space marine in the Navi-Shield Coalition.

"Pass me that '77, would you, captain?"

Gort sipped the Venusian vintage, a full-bodied red with legs to spare. He reached across the table and passed the bottle to the retired admiral, his dad, as the Condor soared across the Milky Way. They returned from Abu-7 with its cargo bays jammed with the stuff.

The venerable space warrior sat at the seat of honour. He poured a glass and raised it to the table. "I may be just an old serviceman enjoying the ride to Venus with my son, Captain Gort, but I raise a toast to him, and all who serve on his ship."

"Here,   here!"

Gort blushed and accepted the kudos, waiting for the murmurs to subside. "Thanks pops, I'd be nothing without you, " he said, and raised his glass in turn. "To the admiral! To freedom!"

Just then the Condor swerved, and Gort spilled his wine. The crimson stain bloomed on the white uniform, and cries of surprise rose like a gale in the banquet room. A shriek of alarm rang over the intercom, the telltale harbinger of hostile alien interplay.

Gort's smile disappeared and he put down his glass. The ship steadied yet the klaxon persisted. He hammered down the com button and spoke in a hurried, urgent tone. "Flack, what's going on over there? I just spilled my drink. This stuff doesn't come cheap."

Flack's reply came quick. "Sorry, but there's a bit of a problem you should know about."

"The problem other than your sudden change of direction?" Gort growled. "I stained my shirt, and dad's dinner is yet to be served."

"Sorry sir, but it seems the course you plotted before the celebration…"

"Go on, what about it?" Gort said, pouring himself a refill.

"Well, it's taken us into Zenorat airspace. Three of their ships are on our tail, and they aren't happy."

Those gathered at the reception looked around the table at the news. Zenora's inhabitant's inhospitality and bad-temper defined them. They didn't take to visitors, and their treatment of foreigners rivalled that of the most notorious foes of the galaxy.

"Son, what's he talking about? You wouldn't have made such an error."

Gort sipped the '77 and looked at his dad square in the face. "My bad, dad, the Condor, sometimes she has a mind of her own."

The computer's nasal voice sang over the intercom. "Evasive maneuvers, evasive maneuvers! Brace yourselves!"

"Dammit!" Gort cried and chugged back his drink. He threw his empty glass against the wall where it smashed into a hundred pieces. "Stupid, stupid, stupid!"

He pushed himself to his feet and stomped toward the door. "Sorry, dad. This was supposed to be a special night. I can't believe I left the ship in the hands of the autopilot."

Gort strode through the corridors of the Condor, muttering to himself as he went. The silver walls were lined with pictures of past captains. There was Maddock, and Grady, both of which he served under. The faces taunted him, magnifying his error. Robison and Urquhart, both before his time, renowned pilots and esteemed warriors both, smiled from the safe confines of their portraits. He mulled over his mistake, cursing his stupidity and vowing to fight the dreaded Zenorats. *How dare they fire on his ship. I'll disintegrate every last one of them.*

The gallery of level-headed captains eased his emotions and his self-anger abated. He swiped the door handle of the command deck and entered. "Flack, tell me what we got. I have a crew to keep alive, and a hold full of wine."

He attempted to wipe at the stain on his chest. "I've already spilled a cup, and don't mean to waste another drop."

Flack, a small, stocky controller with long, spidery arms, stepped aside and with a flourish, beckoned Captain Gort to his chair, a poufy, beige recliner in the centre of the room. Gort sat, and the restraints encircled his appendages, and the helmet lowered. He was thrust into the three-dimensional view of outside, captured from a 360 degree holocam on the dorsal fin of the rocket. Enemy fighters flew in tight formation behind, firing red laser blasts.

Being back at the helm steadied Gort's nerves. He'd captained the carrier for a year now, and was eager to show his dad—the admiral—what he had. Besides keeping him alive, that is. Through the lens of the VR helmet, he surveyed the space around the sleek, golden rocket. Beyond the chasing Zenorats, sat the orange and green planet Zenora. It was beautiful and haunting with its swirling gas clouds above what appeared to be land masses, eroded rivers, and lingering seas. He marveled at how similar matter and geology reacted throughout the galaxy, the patterns repeating themselves at all life-giving, class-A planets. But there wasn't much time for wonder, he had work to do.

"Increase speed to quanzo-level 14." He said. "Stabilize the Holomizer. We'll use the orbital gravity to bolster our escape velocity."

"Copy that, captain." The voice of Flack, sounding more confident now, echoed through the helmet's earphones. "Enemy also increasing speed and matching ours, sir. Shall I enable Evasion Protocol One?"

Something about the hall of past captains sparked an idea, a glimmer of hope in this situation. Maybe there was a simple way out of this, he thought. He steepled his fingers and reclined in the chair.

"Let's try something different, controller. We have bargaining chips aboard. Let's use them, " he said, "open communications to the lead ship."

"Copy that, captain."

"Zenorats in persuit. We regret we have disturbed your zone. I am sending over a gift in hopes it will soothe your opinion of us, and we can abandon this present situation and be on our way without further incident. I would hate for relations to sour more than they already have. Let's put a cork in it, shall we?"

He touched a control on the armrest and gave the order. "Cargo bay, send over a case."

"Affirmative, captain, teleportation of one box of Venusian wine commencing... now."

Captain Gort heard the telltale"zzzzeeerrp" sound confirming the payload was delivered.

He smiled and watched as the first ship behind them slowed. He thought of his next plans, getting out of orbit unmolested and re-joining the party back in the stateroom with his dad and his cronies. His old man had many such tales of adventure, and Gort was keen to regale him with one of his own, how he used diplomacy to get him out of a tough scrape.

"Incoming projectile, sir."

Gort snapped out of his daydream and looked back. The wooden crate rushed through space and smacked them on the rear viewing windows, smashing to bits on the hull. Shards of wood and glass and wine, wasted, undrunk, dehydrated and crystalized in the cold vacuum, scattered to the void and showering the pursuing ships.

"I guess they're not big drinkers, sir."

"Dammit! Evasion protocol, Flack! Do it now!"

***

"Bearing coordinates 555-G, closing gap, Commander."

Caine's left flank reported his status, followed by the right Zenorat fighter pilot. "Igniting booster rockets, blocking lee-side retreat, sir."

Caine snarled. He shifted his controls forward, and the G-force pressed him back into his chair. "Keep the hammer down, boys, we'll destroy these Venusians before they get far. How dare they enter our space."

The Venusians defied all conventions entering Zenorat airspace, eschewing all protocol, in complete disregard for the treatise of 20-90-776, Space-time law. Forgiveness wasn't on the menu today.

"Trying to bribe us with their cheap wine and their words of apology. Unacceptable, " Caine spat, accelerating after the triple-thruster space carrier ahead. "Uncle Zeke didn't die at the hands of these bastarks so we could molly coddle an invasion force over a glass of fermented grape juice."

The searing image of his dad's brother throwing him in the air on his 6th birthday, the last time he saw him before his ship blew up. Years of toil in the rind-mine gave him countless hours of boring work, plotting revenge against the enemy. He joined the Forces, with nothing but his wits and his strength, all fueled by one thing: killing dirty Venusians. Now here was one right in his sights, and his cavalier gesture of bribery sealed the deal. The interlopers would die a brutal, fiery death at his hands.

"On my mark, fire laser mega-cannons, " he cried. "Ready the big boys."

He readied his giant guns and the sensors showed his flank ships did as well.

"FIRE!"

The three ships let loose their fury, and thick angry bolts of light streamed through space, hitting the fleeing ship. A plasma cloud of sparks and debris erupted, and Caine raised his fist in triumph. "Direct hit, " he exclaimed.

The enemy craft plummeted down and veered right, then spiraled in a haphazard slant toward the planet below. Plumes of flame spewed from the craft's engines, its fuel reserves igniting, and its navigation controls compromised.

"Follow it down, boys, " Caine said, adrenaline from battle coursed through his veins, and he ground his teeth. "Next clear shot, take it. I want every last one of them dead."

***

"Controls unresponsive, Captain, we're all gonna die!"

Flack had become unhinged and waved his arms above his head. "Settle down, coward, this thing ain't over, " said Gort, still wearing the holo-helm. "By a long shot."

He thought back to his training days; emergency crash landings 101 was his second-best mark. Crashing on an enemy planet did not necessarily spell death. Maybe its cold, dark grip awaited them afterwards, but it wouldn't come from the crash–not if Gort had anything to do with it.

"Engage tertiary thrusters and brake shields." He stated, watching through the rear helm at the fighters that still chased them. The zig-zag spiral brought his stomach to the brink, but he held on to his dinner and tried to keep his gaze on the horizon of the planet.

"Condor is levelling, sir, " Flack yelled, his voice measured, the note of panic subsiding. "Engines are gone though; we'll have to coast her in."

Gort slapped his hands together and rubbed them up and down five or six times. The landing joystick deployed from the ceiling. "Leave it to me, Flack. I'll bring this bird home to roost. Inform the passengers. This may get rough."

Flack hit the intercom broadcast button and announced to the ship,

"Prepare for emergency landing on hostile planet. Repeat. Prepare for landing."

Gort grabbed the stick and yanked, pulling the nose of the spaceship up, meeting atmospheric resistance at a thirty-degree angle. Flames shot over the cone and painted the viewing windows red. The captain pulled and strained, holding the Condor steady. He shifted his gaze and saw the enemy fall behind. This unprepared descent was too much for most craft. None would attempt such a foolish move unless no other options presented themselves.

"Entering atmosphere, brace for impact."

Alarms screamed, and the emergency brake shields rattled the falling vessel and all within. Gort tore the stick out of its holder, and the Condor held onto a modicum of positive orientation, yet the speed of descent meant only one thing: they were in for a rough landing.

"Land ho!" Gort screamed, and the ship ripped through the orange, leaning branches of a sloped area of land in a forest of curved trees. A cacophony of shouts and the unbridled sound of terror filled his ears as the Condor smashed through the canopy and scored a wide swath through the vegetation. The rocket's fins cut through the thick branches and before long the ship came to a screeching halt.

After a moment of silence and heavy breathing, Gort removed the helmet and rose from his chair, miraculously upright. "Status, Flack. Whatya' got for me?"

"The ship is half destroyed, captain. Navigation and engines gone, all power draining. Casualty reports: none. Cargo was not so lucky, sir. All but one case of wine has been hit."

Flack turned to Gort and shook his head. "You're not gonna like it, sir.

Enemy craft are approaching."

Gort knew there was only one thing to do. "We gotta get out of here now! Bring the wine and get my dad. Let's do this."

***

The trek through the orange forest lasted for hours. A thick canopy shielded them from the hot starshine, and the sparse undergrowth allowed them escape from the chasing enemy. Gort, Flack, and the admiral led the procession, the lower deck men hoisting the last, large crate of wine among them. The landscape curved with flat terrain, covered overhead by layers of tree-limbs and leaves.

Cheeping, flying animals, and flowering plants with heady, perfumed scents dominated the view. A melancholy, buzzed feeling overcame Gort as they traipsed through the flower fields.

"The smell? Can't you smell that smell?" he said. "I think it's making me high."

The admiral grinned with half-closed eyes. "Push on, son, don't let it get to you. Put it out of your mind."

Gort marveled at the stamina of his old man, crash-landed on an enemy planet and hiking through the alien foliage like it was a walk in the park at home. The minions with the wine labored behind, and now and then, the buzz of an overhead craft announced its search pattern. They came to the edge of a narrow valley, and a break in the trees revealed a space ship nestled in dry-dock at an enemy outpost.

Father and son peeked out of the foliage at the rocket below them.

"See that dad, " he said with a wink and a smile. "Our ticket out of here."

***

THE ZENORATS DIDN'T KNOW WHAT HIT THEM. A FURIOUS TEAM OF Venusians dropped out of the forest and took out the guards in a volley of laser fire led by the ferocious fighting of father and son. Gort felt himself driven by an unrelenting need to get the hell out of there. Life had become too complacent, too easy. He'd stagnated under the routine merchant runs and trading missions. His mistake with the autopilot proved that. He wanted to show his dad that he too was a fighting man, a leader who could get results. He had a thirst for life.

They jumped into the ship and engaged the controls. "Strap that case of wine down, boys, we're getting out of here!"

Gort took a moment to survey the dashboard of the alien craft. It was different, yet alike their own. He speculated how they'd become enemies, and what the chance for peace was. They obviously didn't like wine, so there had to be major differences, but still, he wondered. There had to be a better way.

Flack pulled down the giant lever in the middle of the control room and the Zenorat ship hovered above the clearing. "We're ready, captain. All systems go."

"Copy that, Flack. Let's get out of here."

Gort jammed his foot down on the pedal and the stolen craft cut above the tree-line and shot into space.

* * *

"BOGIE ON OUR TAIL AT SIX O'CLOCK, " FLACK YELLED.

Gort grimaced. *Is there no end to this damned conflict!* He dropped the rear laser controls and fired the blasters at the chasing ships. One exploded, but another emerged from the plasma cloud.

It bore down on them, and Gort swerved to the right, then left, then looped-di-looped back over top until the lone gunner was in his sites.

"Fire!" he yelled, and the guns roared, blowing up the last enemy in a huge, fiery explosion.

The crew cheered, and they plowed through the residue of the destroyed ship, and metal shards and burning chard peppered them. The grim look of death gleamed in Gort's eye as they tore through the debris and escaped the planet's orbit. He'd saved himself and his men but killed countless Zenorats. If only they'd accepted his gift, they could have avoided all this bloodshed. After all, were they not similar? Gort hated war and all it stood for, but sometimes people couldn't get their heads out of their asses. They attack when they should just chill. It didn't make sense.

He got up from the control chair and made for the back rooms where the admiral and the other guests hunkered down with the wine. "Good shooting, back there, Flack, you got us from here?"

"Aye aye, captain."

Gort had never been in such a battle, and at one point, death seemed certain. He mourned the loss of the Condor, but his crew and his dad were safe, as was one precious case of the Venusian Vintage '77. He greeted the admiral, stepped up to the grey-haired gentleman and saluted.

"Well sir, what are we waiting for?" he said with a grin. "Crack a bottle open. What's one more gone after all?"

Seacrets

By MA-J

1

THE SEA SPARKLED AS A GIANT MOON ROSE, BRINGING WITH IT THE glimmer of hope Pichon city needed. Its waters were blue. Solène pulled down her mask and walked into the sea.

Three months ago, she came home to find her favorite beach closed off to the public. From what she understood through the news, an accident had occurred at sea miles away. An oil tanker and a leisure vessel collided sometime in February on a stormy night where it not only took the lives of passengers and crew members on the ship, it also created an ecological mess for the nearby coastlines. About six months later, oil from the spillage was still making its way onto the beach of Pichon city. When Solène came back for summer break in May, she joined the volunteers for the cleanup efforts without a second thought.

The beach reopened to the public tomorrow. Tonight, it was hers alone. Her parent's home backed off into a strip of land that lead directly into the public area. Back in her high school days, she used to take Fabien and Adrien swimming and diving at night. Now she lived miles away from the sea for three quarters of the year. Unfortunately, she only had a few hours tonight to enjoy the sea. She barely rested at all over the summer, having spent it helping her hometown after that catastrophe.

Solène emerged from the water with her pouch full. A pale orange Sturgeon moon had risen quite a bit while she was under. It was time to go home. The bells above the door chimed when she pushed it open, jolting her father awake. He had begun to snooze on the cash register but now he smiled. His beautiful daughter had come home from a full day of volunteering down at the beach. She had become such a mature, caring young woman.

A lot like her mother, he thought. She didn't get much rest, yet she looked as bright and fired up as one could be. She came by to help him and Adrien close the store.

-You are the only person I know who catches a cold during the summer.

-And you are the only person I trust to cure me! He grinned.

Adrien could only giggle. Never get in between family members bickering. Her father owned the only garage and marine supply store in town. Adrien was his favorite, and only, apprentice.

The three of them locked up, but they only let him leave after sharing a nice cup of medicinal tea and a bowl of soup. Solène thought if she didn't cure them both at once they would keep catching that runny nose off of each other until she came back for Christmas.

-Should I pick you up in the morning?

-I'll be gone by the time you wake up!

-Why leave so early?

-Because I need the day to move and settle in before class!

-Well, then ... Travel safe!

Adrien left and the two headed up the stairs. Home. Her father went to bed but Solène had one more task to accomplish before dozing off. Even though her mother passed away 4 years ago, most of her equipment was still stored in the house. She used to be a very famous artisan before her illness took ahold of her. Solène took out what she needed and set up on her desk with a lamp. She emptied her little pouch onto a towel in front of her. Shells and stones of all kinds came pouring out. She slowly wiped and cleaned each one of them as thoroughly as possible. She drew out multiple ideas in a notebook at first but settled on this one beautiful necklace. Solène then spent the night trying to apply as much of her mother's craftswomen techniques as she could remember.

The smell of breakfast and coffee woke her up in the morning. She rushed down to find her father already up and about, to her surprise.

- You look so good this morning!

- My cold is gone, my dear! My nose is so clear I can smell my moustache!

His echoing laughter filled the room as he walked away. She sat and ate her weight in scrambled eggs.

- I tried to follow your design as much as I could.

- OH! Thank you ...

Though she had fallen asleep on her desk mid progress, her wire necklace was completed.

-You picked out the most beautiful stones! She held her curly frizzy hair up while he put it on for her. The stone in the pendant is gorgeous at night. It glows.

-I know right! We might have to check the UV levels in this house. The Internet says it's a calcite and willemite stone or something like that! They fluoresce in a tone of green and orange under certain conditions!

Solène was already packed and she boarded her bus before the sun came up. She would arrive sometime around noon after a five-hour trip. Hopefully, she wouldn't be too tired to finish moving in with Sonia.

2

ANTS RAN THROUGH HER LEGS WHEN SHE STOOD UP TO GET OFF THE bus. Her tall, athletic frame didn't do well in cramped spaces. She sat through all five hours with her knees almost up to her chest. Sonia's new car, on the other hand, was spacious enough for her to lounge around. Moving out of the dorms was her idea. The girls went straight to the supermarket to fill their new home with all sorts of goodies. While Solène was gone for the break, Sonia had used her bewitching smile to get help from a few strong classmates. Most of the heavy lifting was already done. The roommates spent the rest of the evening decorating, eating and relaxing in their brand-new apartment on the edge of campus.

The difference didn't matter much when it came to going to class, but this first day of school simply lingered. Solène didn't get to relax at the beach as she planned. She had so much energy to use. She would not sit still.

Her father's curly-haired apprentice chose a table by the coffee place's window. He waved to her from his seat.

-Adrien!

-Sit, how was your first day?

- Not bad... Slow though ...

-Ok ... Well ... your father's shop was broken into yesterday.

-What!

-He is okay! Don't panic ... He reaches for her shoulders ... No one was in the store and we're not sure what they took.

-Why would you leave father alone then!

-Calm down, Miss! Your father sent me... We have a project on a deadline and the mess they made damaged important components for it. I'm here to buy more.

-I don't like this ... Her brows locked into a frown. Her shoulders slumped away from Adrien's embrace.

-Come shopping with me; you know this town better than I do.

The pair roamed about the city. They completed Adrien's to-do list and had dinner together. Before they knew it, night was upon them. Solène dropped off Adrien at his AirBnB and went home with a take-out bag for Sonia. She started her new job this afternoon and she wasn't the type to go home to cook.

Solène walked past an ambulance and a police car parked on the streets to get to her building's front entrance. Her steps slowed down a little bit when she got to her floor; a uniformed officer was standing right at her door.

-Sonia!

-I'm here...

Her weakened voice came from inside.

-What happened?

-I walked in on robbers ...

The paramedics had her strapped on and ready to roll.

-Are you okay?

-I'm fine... They just need to check on me because I got hit on the head.

She explained that neighbors found her lying on the floor with a bleeding wound. Solène stood in her destroyed apartment. They busted in the door. They opened every kitchen cabinet door and pulled out the food. They pilfered cushions, opened the mattresses in both rooms. They even emptied her lingerie drawer. One of them even took off the lid on the back of the toilet. It appeared someone was deliberately looking for something. At the very worst, someone enjoyed making a mess of their home. They took her to the hospital and Solène stood in the mess with questions.

Adrien rushed over to be with her. So much worse could have happened when she walked in on those criminals. Fortunately, they simply rushed her to escape with no intent to harm her. Her head wound was the result of her falling to the floor. That, too, could have produced a very gloomy reality had she not been found in time.

Solène didn't say much but Adrien could tell that she was feeling bad. Maybe she thought if she'd gone home sooner she could have done something. Not true.

3

SOLÈNE SAT OUTSIDE SONIA'S EMERGENCY ROOM AS SHE GAVE HER statements to Detective Rosemond.

Adrien elected to push his return to Pichon city back another day. Solène's father encouraged this decision. Even if he couldn't get everything under control in the store, having someone by his daughter's side was the correct decision.

The girls didn't fall asleep until morning. Sonia was held overnight for observation and Solène didn't leave her bedside at all. Their conversation went from health concerns to baking cookies to thanking the cute neighbor for coming to her aid. Adrien simply sat in a chair by the window and watched. He could tell the ladies were scared out of their minds, yet they spoke as if they were totally fine. It was cute.

Sonia was released sometime around noon. Though she had a head injury that needed sutures, she was healing very well, and she would be okay outside of the hospital provided she came back for a check-up at some point. Adrien was the first to go through the yellow tape even though the girls had come up the stairs before him. They took turns taking a shower as Adrien stood watch from the living room. The roomies then tried to put things back in place in their bedrooms first before moving on to other rooms. They were hoping to figure out what was taken but to no avail.

Solène could not shake this odd feeling.

-If you look for something at some point you have to find it, right?

-Right... responded Adrien.

-So why didn't they stop looking? They went through every room in the apartment! Why...

Sonia was a little puzzled by her question.

-They were still going through our stuff when I got here.

-So they haven't found it then...

Adrien's conclusion sent a cold shiver down the girls back... It meant they might return to find it. Solène broke the sudden silence.

-There is no way I'm sleeping here... I'm packing a bag. We can stay at a hotel for now...

-We don't even have a door per-say anymore, said Sonia staring at the wide-open space where the police tape hung.

Adrien was inspecting the remnants of it barely hanging on to its hinges.

-I can fix that before I leave, he said. Make a to-go bag. I'll take you to the hotel then I'll come back to fix it. You'll have it back up sturdier than ever with brand new locks in the morning.

Adrien dropped them off at the hotel as agreed and went to buy what he needed. The roommates checked in and Sonia called Detective Rosemond to talk to him. He showed up about an hour later.

It wasn't difficult to convince the detective of their conclusion. They shared a coffee in the lobby as they went over their statements with him. Sonia definitely wasn't the target. Detective Rosemond didn't exactly have reassuring news for them either. No clues and no leads, no fingerprints, no CCTV, no this, no that. He had even more questions than answers. Nothing they owned was taken, not even jewelry or their big, new, fancy TV.

Detective Rosemond approved of their choice not to go back before fixing the door. A wise decision, he said. He stood up, right after finishing the bites and coffee he was sharing with them. Solène and Sonia walked him out. Two black vehicles pulled up in front of them as they said their au-revoir.

Armed and masked men came pouring out. They ran back into the hotel. The Detective screamed at people to get away or take cover. Bullets whistled past their ears. Together they rushed through an employees-only door in the shabby hotel's lobby. The young officer fired behind him to deter the strange men. The girls made it through one more door and emerged in a parking lot. Solène crashed onto the side of a car in her rush. Adrien, unbeknownst to them had circled to find a parking spot. They climbed into his beat-up orange Suzuki as more shots were heard. The inspector fired shots over and over again. He emerged from the exit following them but his steps gave in.

-What is he doing?

-Get on detective!

His legs buckled and Solène screamed.

4

HE COLLAPSED FACE-FIRST ONTO THE PAVEMENT. SHE PUT A LEG OUT to rush to his aid but Adrien held onto her jacket and stepped on the gas. The door slammed back in as he sped out of the parking lot.

Two faint pops echoed as they drove away. Sonia didn't dare turn around to look. Solène crumpled into the front seat and couldn't move a muscle. Adrien was the only one who dared take a glimpse in the rearview mirror, still holding onto her hoodie.

Sonia rummaged through her sweatpants' pockets.

-We should call the police. They might think we did this ...

She sniffed back her tears. Adrien slammed on the breaks, screaming.

-No, don't!

-What!

- Did you tell anyone you were at the hotel?

-No, only the detective!

-Then how did they find you?

Sonia was flabbergasted ...

-Are you saying the police sent them?

-Unless you did... What do these guys want from you...?

-From me? ... How do we know they did not follow you from the apartment?

-Stop it!!!

Solène's tears were finally running and this shouting match in the car wasn't helping.

-Both of you could be right! So stop it, someone is dead. Just stop it... She stepped out of the car... Sonia call your stepfather. He is in the police, isn't he? He will know what to do ... I think they are after me...

They needed a breather. Adrien stepped out of the car after they had calmed down. He sat next to her on the sidewalk.

-What makes you think they are after you?

-First, they went through father's shop, then my apartment, now the hotel. It is not that complicated.

-You have enemies? I don't believe it... he joked

- Me neither, said Sonia coming off her phone call. My dad said not to return to that police station but to take the bus to his station. It's three hours away.

-What about the car?

-He said drop the car a block away from the station and get on the bus. He will send for it because it might have some bullets on it or evidence and whatever. He said he would reimburse us for the tickets too.

So the three of them followed her stepfather's direction to the letter. First, abandon the car then head to the bus station. The roommates sat together and Adrien took a seat a row behind. The dimly lit bus filled to about two-thirds of its capacity and departed. Slowly they dozed off one by one as the sky darkened for the night. Solène's mind filled with worries for her father. He'd been raising her alone since high school. A strange illness at the beginning of the school year took her mother away before Christmas. He even took on Adrien when his mother passed away, too, a couple of years later. Now both of them were running for their lives while he was left alone.

Tires screeching woke them. The bus barely managed to come to a full stop without toppling over. Small luggage pieces and belongings flung around. Even passengers were thrown out of their seats.

-I think a creature might have jumped in front of the bus, said Adrien who was barely resting his eyes.

Panic slowly takes hold of the girls, tightly holding on to each other. Solène's attention was elsewhere though. There was something up ahead on the road.

-Adrien... she whispered. I think there are cars in the middle of the road.

-Is it a traffic accident?

Sonia lunged over Solène's thighs, trying to get a peek out the tinted window.

-Oh my God, they found us, she screamed. We need to get out of the bus before they get here.

The three scrambled but managed to hoister themselves out the back window just as the first gunman climbed onto the bus. He went through every row one by one with a flashlight.

-Dorsainvil, Sir, they aren't here.

-Impossible, the device says it's here. I am clearly reading its energy. The Dorsainvil character screamed at his henchmen. Find them.

5

SOLÈNE AND HER FRIENDS CROUCHED TIGHTLY BEHIND THE BUS.

-The longer we are here, the bigger the danger is for these people, Sonia whispered.

Before they could make a move, two armed men found them. A gun appeared near Solène's face. They were quickly encircled. The Dorsainvil character approached.

-You give me headaches, Miss Solène, he said as he glared into her eyes.

She stood as stiff as she could but her hands wouldn't stop shaking.

-The egg please, young lady.

-I don't know what you are talking about.

Dorsainvil glanced at a device he was holding. A purple light pulsated from its screen.

-I believe you are lying to me.

-Why would I be going around with an egg in my pocket?

Adrien plunged for one of the guns. And so did Sonia. Dorsainvil simply stepped back and left the cluster to sort itself out. Shots were fired but Solène escaped into the woods. Sonia had suggested they make a run for the trees. They could hear the highway from their location.

She ran straight at first, never looking back. When she sprinted she could tell Sonia was lunging to, she wasn't so sure about Adrien though.

The woods thickened as she progressed inward. The ground became uneven the further she ventured away from the road. Her boots snagged on something and she lost control. Her ankle gave way and she slid into a small ditch. She crouched there and simply waited. Fast footsteps got closer to her location. She peeked only to find a panting Sonia making her way through. Together, they went to find a secure place to rest her twisted ankle. They settled in the crevasse of a giant, hollow tree. The night grew darker and colder.

The sound of leaves crunching under nearby footsteps got closer. Solène's entire body clenched, working not to breathe heavily. Sonia grabbed a fallen branch and retreated further into the hollow tree trunk. Silence set upon them and the air got heavier. A shadowy male figure bent over to the opening. Adrien reflexively muffled the young women's screams. He came out of nowhere. Sonia's eyes bugged out of her head.

-You.

-Yes, me. Don't scream.

-How did you find us?

His eyes went straight to the glow emanating from Solène's chest.

-I thought one of you was using a flashlight. I saw it in the distance and followed.

Soléne reached for the pendant on her necklace. It had begun to fluoresce as the night got darker. She swung it back under her shirt.

-Are you okay? Did they leave? Solène worried …

-We have a problem. I heard them say they are going to exchange your father for their egg.

Adrien waited for them to react but they sat, motionless.

-I had eggs for breakfast the morning I left Pichon…

-Oh my God, you ate it! ...

They laugh, bemused.

-Girls, this is serious.

-I saw the screen on their device. They are tracking one person, me.

-Which means if we separate, they can't follow all of us.

- I can go back to Pichon, that's where my father is and maybe he has their egg.

-And I can go find my stepfather ... Can you walk? Pichon is still a couple of hours away.

-My ankle is fine. It doesn't hurt anymore. I can go.

They walked together for a while and when they rejoined the road they went their separate ways. Sonia took the road to Colper Town as they originally intended and the other pair headed back to Pichon city.

6

SOLÈNE'S HEAD HUNG DOWN AS SHE WALKED TO PICHON, CLOSELY followed by Adrien. She kept glancing back at her friend heading alone in a different direction. Her stepfather was the assistant director of the federal investigative department over there. He would surely come with help.

They made their way back to town and her store under the cover of a gloomy sky. A shy ocean breeze welcomed them back but Solène's father was nowhere to be seen. She walked through the remnants of the break-in. They went through her belongings in the house and her father's shop. Even her late mother's defunct office space had been invaded.

-What if I actually ate their egg that morning?

-Would you go to all this trouble for a chicken egg? Let's just sleep here tonight and think this through tomorrow.

-My father isn't answering his phone. I think they may already have him.

-We'll find him when we find the egg.

They continued to talk through the night, though they had decided to rest a bit. Solène kept on trying to clean and fix things. Adrien kept going through things, ranting about not knowing what to look for.

Waking to a smell of breath mints and cigarettes strong enough to almost make her vomit, her head was caught with a dark fabric bag. Strong arms seized Solène who had fallen asleep in her father's workshop. She struggled to get free. She kicked her feet out and about. His strength proved to be insurmountable. Dorsainvil's voice called out to get her under control. A hit on the head rendered Solène unconscious before she could free herself.

Her hands were bound behind her back when she came to. She heard the sound of water running in the distance. People were talking somewhere close even though she couldn't make out what they were saying.

-Hello! ... Somebody help!

-Solène, is that you?

Her father's voice brought tears to her eyes. She wiggled herself into a seated position. With her knees, she managed to pull the bag off her head.

-Appa! Are you okay?

-I'll be fine.

The old man sat up against a ceramic wall across the room he was chained to. He looked as though their captors had battered him. The two snuggled together in the damp room. Henchmen then brought in Adrien. He thrashed around, giving them hell. He caught one on the chin and another one in the groin area before being tased unconscious.

A figure called for the man with the device they used on the bus as he approached.

-Dorsainvil, where is it?

-They brought it back with them, sir. We just need to know what it looks like.

A frail gentleman in a purple suit walked in. Everyone else in the room stiffened their stance.

So that's the man who has been hunting me, she thought. No wonder he sends goons to do his bidding. I could have whooped his derriere with one grand battement.

-It was in their store last night sir, she has it with her.

He scowled at her through his glasses.

7

-DO YOU KNOW WHO I AM, MISS SOLÈNE?

-No...

-Maybe that's why you steal from me, hand it over.

-Are you aware that your friends here have killed a police officer?

-Like I care! Here is your father, now give me my egg.

-I had eggs for breakfast ...

His hand landed on her face before she could finish her sentence.

-You do not want to mess with me, young lady.

-Sir...a henchman emerged with a shy voice.

-What!

- Your mother is demanding after you.

He walked away with the lackey who had come looking for him. Solène collapsed on her father's thighs. Her head throbbed. Dorsainvil crouched down next to them as Adrien regained consciousness in the back.

- I have been nice but I guess I no longer have to. You see, Damien, my boss, wants that egg and he no longer has patience.

-But I don't have it!

-Is it possible you really swallowed it? See we track its energy at night. It was with you on the bus and at the store before we went to grab you. That's how we knew you were back in town.

Adrien, tied up, stared at the two in conversation.

-Can you at least tell us what it looks like?

-I have been told the egg carries its mother's colors into the sea until it creates colors of its own. There is no way you mistook it for breakfast, Miss Solène. I'm going back to dismantle your father's store, and if I don't find it; I'm going to have to cut you open to search through your stomach contents.

Adrien would not sit still. Dorsainvil and the others left them tied up with one guard as they went looking for their egg. Solène kept thinking.

-What did I bring with me, Adrien?

-You made a to-go bag back in your apartment.

-I just put toiletries, clothes, and my computer in with the usual things.

-Maybe you have it on you?

-My pockets are empty, they searched me.

  "PssssT"

The muscular man left alone to guard them walked out of sight for a single second. A man in a lab coat appeared just after with keys to their chains, pulling the guard into the caged area with them.

-Fabien! … Is he dead?

-Chloroform … C'mon, let's go.

Together, they snuck through the fish farms facility. The smell of fresh water was a dead giveaway. They avoided workers and cameras as much as they could. Fabien sent them out through some shady pathway. He then drove around to find them with his old jeep. Victorious laughter filled the car as they hurried up a beaten road into the green surroundings.

-It's nice to see the three of you together again. Her father could barely talk now.

Solène took care of her father in the back seat. Fabien drove without lifting his foot off the gas and Adrien kept an eye on the rearview mirror.

-I think he has some broken ribs. He is not breathing properly.

-I think I just lost my dream job but that's okay. We can take him to safety.

-How did you find us?

-I was bringing your father some fresh fish when they took you this morning. I recognized Dorsainvil and followed him back.

-Do they work here?

-He is the new owner's assistant.

-The Damien dude?

-Yeah, the old man was on the boat that crashed earlier this year. You know the one who sprung the oil spill. I heard some of your conversation coming through the vents into my lab.

-I don't have their egg, I don't know what we are going to do, and they keep finding us.

-I beg to differ. I think you have it and I have an idea.

The Jeep continued for a good thirty minutes on tracks in the forest following the river upstream. It turned into the thickest parts of the woods to a cabin the three of them knew well.

8

-AMMA?...

No one answered. The old house didn't seem abandoned. It smelled of fresh woods and spices. Fabien walked in without waiting for an answer. He found his way through easily by opening the windows. Light filled the room exposing very few mismatched pieces of furniture.

-Your mom lives here?

-Yes, she keeps running away from the hospital just to be here so I pulled her out. She is harmless anyways there was no reason to lock her up. I grew up thinking she was delusional, but I don't think so anymore.

Solène helped her father to the couch and sat next to him. She put his head on her thighs and Adrien walked away to find the bathroom.

-What do you mean?

-The things that always made her look crazy to everyone else, I see them now, I hear them, too.

-Technically, this means you have gone crazy, too!

-The paintings in the fish farms and the owner's homes. It's the exact stories people shunned my mom for believing and talking about them in the city. Yet Amma is the only one who was locked away.

-And you think it's related to what they are looking for?

-You've never seen the paintings, but I have. They portray Sirens and sea creatures. Some images are peaceful and warm; some look vengeful and vicious. Clear nights and rainy days and running rivers plague the old man's entire art collection. It's the same story Amma always told us. You remember it!

-About Callione!

-Damien is looking for Callione's egg. He thinks you have it, Solène.

Amma walked in just then with a bucket full of fish she'd caught. She didn't bother to acknowledge their presence. She looked as gracious as Solène remembered her in the past. Fabien was taken away from her right before they started junior high. Social Services deemed her unfit to raise a child and she was taken into a facility for troubled minds.

The legend said Mother Nature sent her daughter Callione here to care for the waters on this island. Because she was kind and naïve, humans kept hurting Callione. She would fall for the evil ones' traps. But her wrath would always accidentally harm the good souls. So she cast a spell on herself. She lost her ability to roam about in this world with us, but she earned the gift of distinction. If you can find your way to her within the waters, a good heart would earn what he came seeking from her in a peaceful and warm embrace. An evil heart, on the other hand, would never find their way out, let alone what they came looking for. She became the siren with two faces. Whichever one you meet was entirely up to who you were and your intentions.

Adrien returned from his bathroom break to join in on their conversation.

-Are you telling me Damien believes in this?

-His family definitely does. They made their fortune with the waters on this island! That egg might really be theirs.

Solène's nostrils flared a bit and her face quirked.

-Even if it's true. It would not be theirs but hers.

Adrien and the others sat through Amma's meal, going over everything Solène did when she came back for summer break. Amma went on to attend Solène's father's wounds, walking him away to another room.

-What if Damien isn't the one who lost it but the old man? Solène said. Dorsainvil doesn't know what it looks like so neither does Damien.

Solène's expression puzzled them both.

-The old man died in the accident, he is definitely not calling the shots anymore!

-But what if he had the egg with him?

Fabien followed along her chain of thought.

-Which would mean it sank with their yacht.

-After the wrath of the sea sank it. Callione is a sea creature; what if she went after them for stealing it? Solène had a sparkle in her eyes.

Adrien almost jumped up from his seat.

-You think you know what it is!

They think I have it because I spent the summer cleaning after that catastrophe. If it washed ashore, a volunteer must have found it. I picked up so much crap from the beach after that ecological tragedy.

Adrien nodded along as he listened to her.

-Do you know what it looks like? Where is it?

Amma walked in on their conversation.

-Here it is! she said, staring. You should take this back.

Fabien and Adrien followed her gaze.

-You should take this back to your father, she said, handing her a bowl.

9

THE SUN SET QUICKLY THROUGH THE OPEN WINDOWS OF THE OLD wooden house. As night fell, the pendant on her necklace glowed, brighter than it ever did before. Amma wouldn't stop staring at it. Solène held on with a firm grip to the now warm necklace on her chest. She used to love making pendants with her mother. Her craftswoman's skills were unmatched by anyone. She felt as if her mother was right there with her. It was the only thing she took away from the beach. Maybe, just maybe.

-Do you know how to find Callione, Amma?

She looked out into the forest through the open window.

-Follow the river. She decides if she'll see you.

Birds slowly stopped chirping and grasshoppers took over the voice of the forest as time passed. Solène and her friends headed into the thick woods where Amma gazed earlier. At first, they walked aimlessly, but the sound of running water guided them. Higher up on a hill behind the cabin, a stream burst through rocks on the mountainside. Quickly, it grew and joined others from far away. It later turned into the river that headed down into Pichon city's estuary.

Fabien looked down the path that closely followed along to its side.

-She said to follow the river, he thought out loud.

He reached for Solène's hand and the three cautiously stepped into its rushing waters. Each carefully placed step took them deeper into the water. Small fish and other creatures brushed their skin as their feet sank into the muddy riverbed. With every stride, the water rose further up their bodies until only their heads and shoulders peeked through.

When they were submerged, an illuminated path appeared in the river.

A warm current engulfed and took them away with it. It flowed fast and erratic at times or slowed down and seemed to stop at different sections until the water got cold again suddenly. It felt like they were floating in space for a few seconds but they were pulled in through a strange barrier into a pocket of air.

As Fabien and Adrien tried to regain their breath, Solène looked on to the modest structure in front of her.

-I guess Callione will see us, she said as she hesitantly took the first steps up the stairs.

A short path guarded by strange stone statues with jeweled eyes led to a structure not bigger than a two-story house covered with algae and moss. As they made their way through, creatures resting on those statues came to life. What they had assumed to be a pocket of air was revealed to be at best a portion of breathable water, so she noted when dangerous fish began swimming toward them. Poisonous stonefish at first, but also pufferfish and many more even Fabien's professional capacities could not help identify. As they struggled to navigate through the swarm of creatures, hellbound on stopping them from taking a step forward; goons come crashing through the barrier, and most likely Dorsainvil and Damien not far behind

-We need to get this egg to safety, now. Fabien tossed his belt to Solène. Use it as an electric fan go straight and don't stop. She will know you mean no harm.

Solène ran into the Siren's castle whilst fanning away dangers. She roamed through the endless number of chambers, adventuring into rooms filled with treasures and carvings and ponds and green nature. She found herself at the center of what felt like a maze. Callione rested on a bed of algae at the bottom of a giant tree trunk in the center of her throne room, whose top Solène couldn't see. Small stone statues of creatures and crevasses where eggs not unlike the one she carried nested decked the walls. A strange path of marbled stone traveled through a pond to her. Solène took one step and columns of water came rushing down from no ceiling into the ponds. Before she could grasp her situation, Callione was staring straight into her eyes. She hovered less than an inch away from Solène's face, her dark and emerald green eyes buried into hers.

10

SOLÈNE HELD IN HER BREATH AND STIFFENED. FABIEN CAME CRASHING through a different entrance closely followed by Adrien. Water poured down the non-existent ceiling even more as the beautiful female creature hovered a few inches off the ground, traveling to Fabien first, then to Adrien. She seemed to smile to Fabien like she knew exactly who he was. But her eyes swayed to an orange shade when she extended her hand to help Adrien back on to his feet. Solène stared, stunned.

-I brought your egg back.

Solène's voice carried no strength. Her legs could barely hold her up. A strange feeling traveled her stomach as Callione floated back to her. Her hands fumbled with the pendant.

Damien emerged from behind Fabien at this moment.

-I knew you had it, this entire time.

His gun was raised to Fabien's temple as he leered around.

- Adrien, please fetch it for me.

He staggered to her to retrieve the egg. Solène stepped back.

-It's over Damien; I'm giving it back to Callione.

- You have no idea what this egg is capable of. Give it to me now or your friend is gone.

-Adrien!

Adrien launched for the egg, ripping it from her hand. Her eyes widened as he stood up straight, no longer looking beat from the earlier encounters.

-Are you telling me this rock is the reason I've been babysitting you!

-Did you do this, Adrien! Fabien's eyes turned devil red, but the threat of Damien's weapon prevented him from moving.

A knot built in her throat, as she could not grasp the sudden development.

-Let's go, Adrien. If you don't talk to her, she can't harm you. We can heal my mother now.

- Callione! he uttered. I return this egg to you in exchange for eternal life.

She turned to listen. Her dread hair lightly resting on her shoulders and her mesmerizing tangerine eyes set upon him. The Siren opened her hand to him, in which he placed the egg.

-Thank you … she murmured

-What are you doing? Damien, angry, tried to go after him.

Water burst through the ponds as dreadful screams echoed in the throne room. Fabien crept over to Solène and the two curled up on the floor as more of the sea creatures from outside filled the room. Callione caught Damien by his throat and hoisted the small man to her eye level. Her eyes turned back to the emerald green shade they were at first.

-You are not welcome here!

-I just wanted an egg for my mother. Adrien said it would heal her, please.

She let him drop to the floor and slid to the two crippled in the corner.

-Thank you, she said, as she placed the egg back into the nest in a crevasse right over their heads. Let me help you leave.

The creatures had gone silent but the curtains of water kept pouring. Soon enough they were engulfed in its glistening blue waters and taken back into the warm stream that brought them in.

Solène's eyes opened to find them washed up on the riverside a few meters away from the fish farms junction into the river. Downstream, Damien staggered out of the water as Dorsainvil hurried to take him away. Sirens could be heard approaching in the distance.

His gaze no longer seemed demonic.

A week had gone by and the two had held on to their story. Damien was looking for a necklace Solène's mother was commissioned to design. He thought she'd been wearing it and it belonged to his dying mother. Unfortunately for him, she'd passed away while he was chasing them down in the river.

When a warrant for Damien's arrest came, he was found dead in his mother's bedroom. There was no one to say the contrary. The current had taken Adrien away. In truth, he had asked for eternal life, not immortality. Of them all, he was the only one to have met her tangerine eyes. She had her way with him. There was no need to say anything about Callione.

Monstrous creatures of this earth deserve protection, too.

A Stop In Time

By Ali-John Chaudhary

IT WAS JUST ANOTHER DAY. JEREMY PEEKED AT HIS SCHEDULE AND HAD a busy day ahead of him. He had just rejected another person who pitched the idea of yet another schedule that was supposed to optimize a person's day. How many people had he seen that had hoped to be innovators, who, truth be told, were just replicating an otherwise old idea. Been there, done that. It's those people Jeremy had to sift through. The unremarkables. The people that tried to capitalize on another person's idea. No money to be made there. He had been recruited by Huntington Products in their marketing wing. He had become so that he was able to immediately tell if a product had potential or not. In a short interview, he would know instantly if and what products would fly boldly or crash to the ground, costing the company dearly in time and investment. This was one of those occasions.

Jeremy put his hands in front of him, stood up, walked from his desk. As he rose, it was obvious that he had a certain stature that made him all the more impressive, at 6 feet and 2 inches, with dark brown hair that was slicked back, and with blue eyes whose stare could pierce through concrete. He regularly wore a blue business suit. The color of possibility, a tailor had once told him. And today, there were little possibilities to be had. They had heart, and they knew their stuff. But as with so many products, it has seen the light of day many times over.

"Thank you very much for your exciting sales pitch. You have a strong sell, and you can easily tell you know your product inside out. But the question remains, how is this any different than all the other schedulers on the market?"

"Well, you see, we include habit forming exercises, and innovative questions to boost motivation…"

"Yes, and? I've seen this already before. Had you guys come to me 10 years ago, I would have seen potential for this. Now, everyone and their cousin is doing the same thing. You guys missed the boat. I'm afraid we at Huntington Products will have to take a pass."

"But Mr. Mansfield, we think you're missing the point of what this could mean for your company!"

"Such as?"

Jeremy gave them that same piercing stare, which took the wind out of the Freely brother's sails. It became apparent that they could add nothing more, as Jeremy had already made his decision. And as great as a product can be, Jeremy had exposed them to the awful truth: They were too late.

"Now gentlemen, if there's nothing else, I have a 10:15 appointment."

Jeremy raised his arm and took to show them the door. It was too late. Most people didn't know it, but the product marketer always gave them their best chance at convincing them, even right at the end. It was not his habit to use his intimidating stare. But he had people to see, and if people couldn't prove him wrong, then there was no time left to waste with them. Each meeting that was rejecting a product was keeping a next person from booking and seeing Jeremy, potentially allowing them to approach another product marketing company that could see the potential in what they had. He had to act fast. And when he knew, he knew. Jeremy's track record at finding innovative products was well known, if not legendary. He grew to understand that his time was precious. And people at the office also knew not to cross him.

Jeremy was an eccentric. Always living intensively in both work and play. So much so that when his secretary had accidentally double booked two clients at the same time, he went through a whirlwind of a rage that ended in objects thrown, words that couldn't be taken back, and Jeremy storming out of his office for the remainder of the day. He became just as notorious for his excesses in anger as his genius in identifying the next big thing. The higher ups reminded Jeremy to play nice. Indeed, he had learned that you catch more flies with honey than you do with vinegar. In the next few months, Jeremy came to know everyone's birthday in his work section, and made it a point to get them a gift each year. It was not much, but Jeremy came to turn the tide that was building against him. People knew to let him do what he did best, and step out of his way when he would lose his cool.

Today wasn't one of those days where composure was to be lost.

"Sir, Mr. Mortimer, your 10:15, has just arrived."

"Thank you, Claire. Let him in."

Jeremy studied the demeanour of everyone, and could tell who was in pain, who is determined in their steps, and who was completely unsure of themselves. That is why when Mr. Mortimer strolled into his office, he was left wondering just what type of crazy he was bringing with him.

After all, no one really one dresses up in a vertical lined ringmaster suit. All that was missing was the tall hat. The man in purple and white stripes immediately approached Jeremy and shook his hand wildly. Instantly, he noticed his step was unusually wobbly. Almost as if he had taken a drink prior to his meeting. Curiously, the product marketer had concluded that this was not the case.

"Pleased to meet you Mr. Mansfield. I'm Mortimer. James Mortimer. I'm certain that you would be just the right person for the product I have in mind!"

"Right down to business, then. Shall we?" Sharp and to the point.

With a wave of his hand, Jeremy guided Mr. Mortimer to sit.

"I see you have something with you. I'm assuming this is what you want to show me?" he pointed at the silver briefcase.

"Yes! Yes it is! But first, I wanted to comment on your office. I can see you've worked quite hard to get to where you're at, Mr. Mansfield." Numerous awards adorned Jeremy's office, which he came to acquire yearly. It only served to further his reputation.

Jeremy, flattered, yet impatient soon rose to his feet.

"Look, if you're here just to comment on my office, I've got better things to do!"

"Quite the contrary, my dear lad. That's exactly my point! You've taken some time to acquire all this, to get to where you're at, with your station in life. In fact, I'm venturing to assume that, like all of us, you'd like to have more time. Isn't that true?"

Finally, back to business. "Wouldn't we all? Now what is it you want?"

Mr. Mortimer, soon sat back down and opened up his briefcase. In it, was a small machine, a ten inch cylinder, that looked like a large bulk coffee can.

"What is it?"

"Rather than telling you, Mr. Mansfield, how about I show you?"

Upon closer inspection, the can had knobs and levers to it. It looked like something out of a cyberpunk movie.

Mr. Mortimer, inserted a key on top of the can, that soon woke it up. Immediately, it started spinning on its axis, and turned on itself like a musical box, with lights that swirled through its various windows. Mr. Mortimer rose what looked to be an arm on the machine, that acted as a lever, that created a sudden surge in Jeremy's office. Lights flickered, and then nothing.

"Ok, what just happened?"

"Why don't we step out of your office to see?"

Not used to getting suggestions like this, Jeremy begrudgingly complied.

"If this is a way to impress me, Mr. Mortimer, you should know that..."

"Just open your door, Mr. Mansfield. That's all you need to do."

Jeremy stepped near to his door, put his hand on the cold metal door handle, and turned.

Dead quiet.

All was still, and by all, this meant every single movement. His secretary, nearby, typed on her computer, with her hands etched in mid-air. Another, Harold the local mailboy, pushed his cart through the department, only no movement came.

"Hey! What's going on, everyone?" Jeremy walked out, and put his hand on his secretary's shoulder. Still no movement. Jeremy even walked further, and looked into various cubicles, only to see people sitting at their computers, transfixed to their screens, frozen like statues. Jeremy even looked at the clock on the wall. It said 10:22am, with the seconds hand firmly in place. Looking at his wrist, his timepiece still continued to move.

Jeremy walked back to his office, saw Mr. Mortimer, with his arms at ease, outstretched, resting on his couch. Picking up speed in his pace, his eyes locked on him, Jeremy grabbed Mortimer by the collar and pulled him up. "What is this?"

Mortimer thrust his hands up to his face, and uttered, with a calm voice. "Just what it looks like. Now, you can have all the time in the world at your disposal. This machine will see to that. Isn't that what you wanted, Mr. Mansfield? Jeremy? A revolutionary product that will change the world? Well, here it is."

Jeremy let go of his grip, and Mr. Mortimer soon took back his seat.

With a deep breath, the product marketer finally spoke: "Ok. So how do we shut this off?"

"Ah, yes. Here is how it's done…"

And within a few moments, ambient noise had soon returned, as did the comings and goings and voices behind Jeremy's door. "You see? All is well."

"How much are you asking for this?"

"Of course, such a machine is priceless. But I would want you to try it out, and see what you feel this is worth. I will be in touch with you in a few days, to discuss a monetary value. Here is my card."

And with that, Mr. Mortimer got up, shook hands, and soon after left the office, in just the same strange way as he had walked in.

Jeremy was left with a mixture of excitement and revolt. How could such a strange man have created such a machine? In any case, he was dead set on continuing to see just how he could make use of it. He remembered how Mr. Mortimer had shown him, he entered the key, waited for the light to turn on, of which it soon did, he pressed the lever up, followed by his office quickly turning sombre for a few moments, before the lights came back on. Jeremy walked out of his office, and explored everyone who was present in the department. It was like they had become statues of themselves, yet still alive. Warm to the touch, they were still in their own world, and yet Jeremy was able to move freely, out and about, and continue on while the rest of the world held still, as if holding its breath. It was then that inspiration struck him.

The product marketer soon returned to his office, and went through some of his neverending paperwork. What felt like a few hours, the clock was still stuck at 10:33am, the time at which it had originally frozen into place. Jeremy was delighted at the thought of being able to accomplish so much at a given time. He felt wonderful with everything frozen like this. And if he didn't achieve much, it didn't matter, as he would just pull the lever, and presto! He was already having scenes of empowering moments race through his mind, giving him a rush of power. His productivity would go through the roof!

He had to see what the real world looked like. Jeremy rushed to his feet, and with the same level of intensity as before, he rushed to his office door. But his left leg decided otherwise, and hit his coffee table first, which started a domino effect. His table moved, pain shot up his knee, and a feeling of horror and dismay washed over him as his time device fell to the floor, and snapped the lever well off. Shocked, and surprised, Jeremy reached down to collect the machine and its lever. He also noticed that it was slightly cracked, due to striking the floor.

"What the hell is wrong with me?" Jeremy quickly sat down, and tried putting the pieces where they were supposed to go, but it became painfully apparent that he was not the handyman that this machine needed to return to its optimal state. A look of horror washed over Jeremy's face as he realized that he could be stuck in this place, rather, this moment, forever. "Maybe there would be an automatic return to real time, " he thought. But he had already been several hours on frozen time, and still no sign of returning to otherwise what was normal. What was he going to do? Would he live all alone and die in this hellish limbo, a man completely alone in the world?

No. He would not allow himself to go down that route. A surge of anger coursed through him. Had Mortimer given him a shoddy product? In a sense, this was good that it happened now, as he would certainly want to avoid this happening to any potential customer. Yes, he knew that he somehow had to get back in touch with Mr. Mortimer, and have him fix this. But would he be alive? As in moving back and forth, and able to speak back to him? Or was he frozen just like the rest of them? There was only one way to find out. He would have to meet with him.

"Where's that card?! Ah! Here it is!"

Jeremy pulled out his cell and dialed. "Wow! Technology's so advanced that it even works in frozen time." He tried twice, three times, but to no avail. He looked further at the card, and saw what looked to be an address. "Better be there, Mortimer", thought Jeremy. He grabbed his coat and threw his machine in a backpack. The product marketer was going to face the frozen world, for the very first time.

Stepping outside was like walking into a still photo. Everyone and everything was paused in place. It made for easy travelling for Jeremy, who luckily was still able to use his phone's GPS system to get to Mr. Mortimer. Jeremy passed street after street. He knew that he could get there in about half an hour. Best to not drive when in these conditions. One never knew just when the road would end or be blocked.

Walking downtown was one of those rare moments that would allow Jeremy to actually enjoy the heart of the city with no noise. In fact, he actually felt at peace, at a time and place where near chaos ensued. Listening to the quiet seemed to sharpen the product marketer's other senses, particularly the visual. His gaze combed the highrises, and actually looking through the windows of whatever store he would pass by was a sharp contrast to gliding by in his car. It was easy for his eyes to take the sights in while walking. Something was odd. Could it be? Through a window, a silhouette seemed to move, breaking the stillness of the environment. Jeremy stopped his pace, only to focus further. Was his mind playing tricks on him?"Were we meant to perceive people when there were none?" Such were the questions that he pondered over. It was then that something struck Jeremy's foot, throwing him off balance, just enough for him to catch himself before falling. His gaze reached down, to see what looked to be one, two, three bodies. Jeremy crouched down to take their pulse. All cold and dead. He counted two more a few feet further ahead. Gazing at his environment, nothing seemed out of the ordinary. A sick feeling suddenly washed over Jeremy. Could it be that these people were others, like him, stuck in time limbo? He would have to ask Mr. Mortimer, IF he ever saw him again. Best to be on his way if he was to get his answers.

A feeling of dread ran through the back of Jeremy's mind. Would he meet the same fate as these people? How could he possibly do any better than those that came before him? No. He forced himself to push those thoughts away from him mind. Just as he was about to walk way, the silhouette he had seen earlier, through the store glass, returned. Jeremy came to life and ran towards the door. He entered the department store, only to see the figure run deeply farther into the back. Like a cat chasing a mouse, Jeremy tried to get closer, but the mysterious person was just too fast. Either that, or they knew the surroundings inside out.

"Hey! I know you're here. I saw you from outside! I just want to talk! Please!"

The product marketer was only met with silence. He ran feverishly through the store, until he had to stop and catch his breath. In between breaths, he let out again: "I just wanted to talk."

Looking back at his watch, his time timepiece was still moving forward. He noticed he had been searching for well over 15 minutes now. But if Mr. Mortimer was able to move about, who's to say if he would stay where he was at for very long? Jeremy exited the building, walked along the sidewalk, and made another call to the vendor of his time machine.

"Hello, this is Mr. Mortimer, at your service! What can I do for you?"

"Mr. Mortimer! Thank goodness I was able to contact you! There's something wrong with your machine! Can you fix it?"

"Ah yes, Mr. Mansfield! I trust that you are getting things done with all your free time? What's wrong with it?"

"It broke, and I can't return to regular time!"

"Where are you now?"

"About 10 minutes from your office."

"Come and meet me here. I'm certain we'll figure it out!"

Jeremy ran like a madman, and made it to Mr. Mortimer's office in a record 7 minutes.

When Mr. Mortimer opened the door, Jeremy handed him the machine with its matching pieces.

"Hmm. I don't think this will be too hard to fix. You certainly are in a bind, stuck in time like this. Of course, there is a matter of payment for repairing this."

"Anything you want."

"Anything? I haven't even told you what the price is, yet."

"Just get it fixed, so I can come back to normal time. We both know I'm good for it."

Mr. Mortimer rubbed his thick mustache, side to side. "Tsk tsk. Mr. Manfield. These types of payments are unheard of, normally, but because of extraordinary circumstances, I will tell you this. In exchange for fixing your machine, I would like a memory of yours."

"What do you mean, a memory? I don't have time to recount my life to you, here!"

"Oh, but that's not what I meant. You see, as an inventor, I've crafted several different machines for different uses. This one over there, for instance, will allow me to take a pleasant memory from you, and a year of your lifespan, and keep it for my own personal use."

Jeremy fell momentarily silent. Finally, he said, "That's the exchange? I don't believe you!"

Mr. Mortimer's expression grew stone cold and cross. In a stern voice, he said, "Well, if you prefer to turn down payment, you can always return to your office, and live out the rest of your life in frozen time. You'll have an eternity to think about your choices there."

Thoughts raced through Jeremy's mind. What choice did he have? And from the looks of Mr. Mortimer, he seemed to be dead serious. Whatever game was going on now, he had to play it, to get to the next step. He turned to look back towards the vendor.

"Agreed."

"Good, now all we have to do is get you this headband on, like so, and I will turn on my machine like this."

Mortimer cranked up an old engine with his hand, and turned the switch over itself, until the engine started. Like a Christmas ornament, small lights burst alive, and started to blink. Jeremy stared, transfixed at them. It was as if the lights were consuming him, and he couldn't help but to look. His mind brought him to think back to when he was 7 years old, as his father pushed him on a swing. It was a wonderful day spent with the family, and one of the few days in which Jeremy had a good time with his dad, before he fell prey to alcoholism.

The lights suddenly died down, and Jeremy was back in Mr. Mortimer's office.

The vendor now took off the headband from Jeremy's head, and turned off the engine. The machine, which looked slightly like a lantern, died down.

"What just happened?"

"I took one of your prized memories, as agreed upon, in exchange for fixing your machine. Of course, you'll live a year less, but that shouldn't bother you too much."

Try as he might, Jeremy felt he could not remember a memory he previously had. It was like there was a white space every time he tried to think of it. Sensing what Jeremy was doing, Mr. Mortimer reassured him. "Trust me. It's completely gone. Now, let's fix this for you!" He smiled. A few minutes later. "There you go! Good as new! Now, please don't drop it again, and be careful in pulling the lever up or down. The crack on the side shouldn't interfere in its proper functioning."

"I guess I should say thanks".

"You guess? Mr. Mansfield, you have possibly the most important human invention ever created, and you doubt to thank me? I'm disappointed."

"So, what do you want for this machine?"

"I still think it's too early to discuss that. How about if I speak with you on monday morning?"

"Alright." Jeremy stood up, slightly dizzy, but soon was able to recompose himself.

Given the circumstances, whoever the product marketer had booked in would take a back seat to Mr. Mortimer's invention. He soon approached the door, turned towards the vendor, and asked, "Why are you selling this? You could live the good life just by having this all to yourself."

"I have my reasons. See you on Monday."

Jeremy walked back to his office the same way he came. After all, this is what creatures of habit do. He found that walking helped to further stop the dizziness. The product developer walked back at a pace that allowed him to take in more of the downtown core. He strolled in front of and past the dead bodies, who seemed pretty harmless by now. He remembered he had forgotten to ask about them. Jeremy reflected on Mr. Mortimer, who undoubtedly was a sly salesman. He knew he would be hooked on the machine as of day one.

His thoughts soon brought him to other matters. It felt good to know that he could just put his life on pause, and that this would be the new reality for him. He could just see the possibilities: Stretch out his vacation time, be more productive at work, pause to observe more details. Study the people who came to his office. It felt good. And he felt good, despite what had just happened. In a sense, he was glad that Mr. Mortimer had declined to discuss financial matters with him. After all, Jeremy was not in his best state, nor was he on his own turf. Those were two factors that had to remain constants in the marketing producer's professional life. It didn't take long to reach his office building, and then his office. Upstairs and back, he took the machine out of his bag and put it back onto his coffee table. He stared at it, and wondered what was holding him back from putting it in full gear. Taking a seat down on his couch, his head thanked him for the slight rest. His hands approached the machine, and he inserted the key. He wondered if it would start or not. He was just about to push the lever up, until he heard a noise.

"What was that? The door to the department?" he thought.

Jeremy rose up, and stepped out of his office, alarmed, his head turned and investigated where the sound came from. He looked around, but all he could see were cubicles and office desks.

"Hello", an unfamiliar voice spoke out.

Jeremy's body stiffened, and he jumped back, startled by an unexpected voice.

"Who are you?"

"My name's Kate. I saw you looking at me through the window. You walked back in front of the store. I was able to follow you here."

"Why'd you follow me?"

"For the same reason you tried to find me. I wanted to see if there were others."

"So, you have one of the machines too?"

"Yes. But you should know, Mr. Mortimer is much more dangerous than he lets on. This time limbo, ever notice how good it feels? That's what he's hoping for. That you get hooked on it. He

doesn't just sell that machine you and I bought, he sells you the addiction. Then, when you're at your weakest, he tries to steal your memories. I can't even begin to tell you what he's taken from me. One thing's for sure, we age a lot faster here than in the real world. 3 times over."

His head spun, and his gut reacted to the words as if he had found a hidden treasure.

"There's so many questions I want to ask you…"

"First, let me see your machine. If it's anything like mine, then maybe I can help you out of this." Who else could he trust? It was strange that she was willing to help him first, before helping herself. But the product marketer chose to ignore this. There was nothing else he could do.

Jeremy soon sat on his couch, and invited Kate to sit in front of him, which she did. He showed her the mechanism with the key, and the lever, and Kate confirmed the flickering lights. Both laughed as if understanding the intricacies of an inside joke.

The two sat back, at ease. Jeremy introduced himself, and both started to talk.

"I saw you staring at the dead bodies."

"Well, it was enough to startle anyone. Do you know who they are?"

"As a matter of fact, I do. I don't know if you noticed, but a great deal of them all had wrinkles on their faces, and white hair."

"I hadn't, no." Just then, Jeremy realized he forgot to ask Mr. Mortimer just who they were.

"They are us! Like you and I. One of them spoke to me before he died, and said his entire memory had been stolen! He just wanted his life back, the poor old man!"

"Wait! Are you saying Mortimer sucked him dry of his memories?"

"Yes! In exchange for a working machine. Only, the machines are made to break easily. He was expecting you to call, and like us all, you bit the hook. It'll only break again, like mine, which is why I'm here!"

Just then, Kate then did the unexpected. She pulled something from her pocket. Jeremy looked down at the barrel of a gun.

"Hand it over, and nothing bad has to happen."

"What? You want this? After everything you said? Why?"

"Mine broke down a few weeks ago, and I have almost no more memories to pay to get it to work. Yours will do just fine!"

Kate got up, grabbed his time-stopping machine, and threw it in her own bag.

"If you try to follow me or find me, I'll shoot. You've been warned."

And with that, Kate left Jeremy's office, and was about to walk out of the department, when Jeremy thought to follow her, despite her warning.

Kate's gun fired its first deafening round, then its second, and a third. Jeremy could do nothing but grab the floor and take cover. She was dead serious, and desperate, he thought. All he heard was the door slam, and Kate taking the elevator back down. He soon got back up, and was about to run after her, but reason got the best of him: he didn't want to risk getting shot in time limbo.

"Damn it! What the hell am I supposed to do now?" Jeremy was at his wit's end. With his machine gone, and stuck in frozen time, there was no way he could reverse this. Where would Kate go? Jeremy paced around his office, taking in just what she had said. There was no way that he could remain in frozen time forever, if he was aging at triple the rate, like Kate said. How long had Kate been in limbo? Clearly, she was addicted to the feeling of stopping time. Jeremy had to admit that there was a rush at stopping and starting back normal time. But to say he would be addicted was a stretch. In any case, he had to think. The only person that could likely help in getting his machine back was Mortimer. But what would he ask of him this time? More memories? Another year? The thought of asking the washed up carnival ringmaster made him gag. But what else could he do? Who knew if there were more people alive or not, let alone in this city. Jeremy swallowed his pride, and decided to dial the number.

"Yes, Mr. Mansfield?"

"There's been a...bit of a problem. Can I come over?"

"Yes, I guarantee all my products. What seems to be the issue?"

"I just got a visit from Kate, and she seems to know you quite well."

"I see. No need to say more. I'll be right there".

Mr. Mortimer arrived exactly 20 minutes later, briefcase in hand. His demeanor was more decisive and sure of himself. In sharp contrast to his relaxed and aloof attitude seen earlier.

He spoke first. "What happened? What did she tell you?"

"Enough to know that you're not exactly selling the machine to us, but rather making us dependent on it."

"That's preposterous! If that was the case, do you seriously think I would go through all this song and dance just to hook you? I could well find anyone on the street for that!"

Jeremy said nothing. This was a man who came prepared for any and all answers. He knew this wasn't the time to discuss this, and that further problems needed to be dealt with. Jeremy explained what happened to Mr. Mortimer, with as much detail as possible.

Mr. Mortimer rubbed his mustache, thought for a bit, and said, "Ok. Here's what we'll do. Jeremy, I usually put a tracking device in each of my items. I don't often use them, but it's a way to know who has what, and how far they are used from the point of sale."

"And a way for you to reuse and resell your machine to the next unsuspecting buyer" thought Jeremy.

Out of his briefcase, the vendor pulled out what looked to be a remote control for a wireless toy, only it had a 5 inch screen with green dots on it. "You see that one? That's her, and... wait!"

"What? What is it?"

Mr. Mortimer's face went white, then beet red. His face tight, and his eyebrows lowered. His mood suddenly changed. In a fit of rage, he shouted out, "Blasted! She has my briefcase! She waited for me to leave, walked right up to my place of work, and stole my briefcase!"

Jeremy thought fast, and put his hand on Mortimer's shoulder. "I'm sorry to hear that. No good businessman should go without his briefcase."

"Indeed. In doing business, no self-respecting man should be without one, or in my case, several."

"So let's help each other. I help you find your briefcase, and you help me find *my* time stopping machine. You can't do this alone, Mortimer!"

Turning his head towards Jeremy, the vendor simply responded, "You're right. But remember, it's not *yours* just yet."

Jeremy and Mr. Mortimer soon exited the department and the building with a newly found resolve. Both wanted their belongings bad enough. The vendor pulled out his tracking device, and Jeremy made sure to pack his own pistol, in case Kate dared to pull out her own again. He wasn't going to be had a second time.

"Mr. Mansfield, she is about 8 blocks east from here. My tracking device puts her at 304 Industrial avenue. She is likely in a warehouse. What could she be doing?"

Upon arrival, Mr. Mortimer had indeed proven right. Jeremy noticed that they were closing in on a building that lay in the industrial quarter, abandoned. The vendor was just about to enter, until Jeremy put his hand on his shoulder. "We shouldn't just walk in from the front door. Let's take the back door!"

"Indeed. A good idea."

Jeremy was able to easily and quietly wrestle open a side door that would allow them a more stealth entry. As the two walked through the warehouse, they were both able to remain discreet, making sure not to gather Kate's attention.

Several feet in front of them, Kate was sitting on a blanket, she tinkered with what looked to be Mr. Mortimer's open briefcase, and a machine not unlike the one that had taken Jeremy's childhood memory from him, headband and all. Beside her, was the other machine that looked to be the same time stopping machine as that of Jeremy's. And still, another machine lay on the blanket.

"Mortimer, I recognize the first two, but what's the third one?"

"No need to concern yourself with that!"

Jeremy turned around, and faced Mr. Mortimer. "If we came all the way here to reclaim my machine, and put ourselves in harm's way, I have the right to ask what that blasted machine is for!"

Mr. Mortimer turned left and right, with a hand on his forehead, before finally giving in. "Alright! That machine creates inter-dimensional portals. I use it to communicate with beings from another dimension. I don't know what she wants from that...but it's certainly nothing good. Do you have your pistol with you?"

"I do."

"Then let's approach her from behind, that way, we get the element of surprise."

Carefully able to get close behind Kate, the two men were just a few feet from behind her, as Kate was busy working on the third machine. She finally pressed a button, and gently posed the machine to the ground.

With his gun pointed at her, Jeremy spoke first. "Time's up Kate. Hand our stuff over!"

Startled, she reached for her own gun.

"I would advise against that Kate! Did you think you could just take the machines without

consequences?" Mr. Mortimer said.

Kate laughed. "In a sense, I'm glad you're here! This all started with you! I've been studying you for some time now! You probably didn't know it, but I had a lot of time on my hands and was able to put up working spy cameras all around your office."

"You fiend! How dare you spy on me and my private projects?"

"It was the only way to know your motivations, Mortimer! Now, I understand why you do what you do! I only want what's mine. I want my memories back, and my stolen years too! And now, I've found a way to do just that!"

Soon after its initial activation, the third machine awoke at Kate's feet, and shot a beam of light. From that beam, a rip in the very fabric of reality seemed to appear in mid-air. A green light blasted through, and a hungry, foreign, soul-piercing scream coursed through the entire warehouse.

Jeremy asked, "What was that?"

"The creature. It's awake, and it wants to feast!" Mortimer said.

Kate spoke again. "Mortimer, I think I know just what that thing is begging for. And I'm going to give it just that." The woman feverishly grabbed at her gun.

Jeremy fired a round in the air. "Don't do it, Kate!" There was no way she was going to throw the time stopping machine to that thing.

As if able to read his mind, Kate responded. "It's not your machine that it's after. It's this!" Kate pointed to the machine with a headband. "It wants this, and Mortimer knows it!"

Just as Kate pointed her gun to the memory machine, another pistol fired a shot, hitting the woman square in the stomach. Jeremy turned around and saw Mr. Mortimer's smoking weapon. Kate fell to the concrete floor, and dropped her pistol.

"What'd you do that for? I thought the guns were only to be used as a last resort!"

"Yes, and I'll resort to anything to protect those memories. Including yours, Jeremy!"

Kate sat up painfully, as Mortimer slowly approached his machines. "Ask yourself why he wants the memories so badly, Jeremy. Ask yourself why..." With a swift upward movement of his arm, Mortimer came crashing down on the back of her head with the handle on the gun, making her fall back to the ground, unconscious.

"That's enough out of you!" Mortimer added.

The creature from the other dimension edged closer and closer to the opening. A fleshy mucus colored tentacle with suction cupped openings seemed to permeate along it's entire body. It looked faintly like an octopus, except its tentacle had small mouths, all of them were making a chorus, as if demanding to be fed. Was this what Kate was alluding to?

The tentacle approached Mortimer, and he, it. Both were in recognition of each other. If what Kate said was true, Mortimer must have been feeding the creature memories. "But what for? What could the creature possibly give him, that he would want?" Jeremy looked back at his time-stopping machine. And then, it suddenly dawned on him, as he answered his own question. "In exchange for knowledge in how to build the machines." That was the mutual arrangement between the two!

It was now or never. Jeremy took a step forward, took a deep breath, and with his last remaining bullets, fired his gun onto the memory machine. "I hope you're right, Kate."

The machine exploded into pieces, and dismantled right in Mr. Mortimer's hands. A bluish hue emerged from the wrecked machine, spewed colors of all kinds, and rose like a rainbow colored whirlwind, blowing in all directions. Years of memories and lifespans flew up in the air, with many colored strands that ventured close to Kate's head, until finally they entered through her ears. Kate quickly rose up, as if being given an electrical jolt. Her eyes widened, having the feeling of meeting an old friend. A bright yellow stream lunged towards Jeremy. It reached him, and entered, in its turn, through his ear canal. Kate pulled herself, and the time-stopping machine, out of the way, and nearer to Jeremy, for cover.

The rest of the memories, seemed to disappear up in the air, while others were grabbed by the tentacle, seemingly satisfied at finally being able to feast. Jeremy had been right to listen to Kate.

Mortimer turned back to the product marketer. "What have you done? You've ruined my life's work! I'll kill you both!" And he pointed his gun angrily towards Kate and Jeremy. The product marketer was pointing his gun, empty, back at him. It was one of the last things Mortimer would ever see.

Behind him, the tentacled being moved frantically, as if hungry for more. It grabbed what little memories it could, and sucked at the strands and inhaled them somehow with the little mouths around its large tentacle, until no more colors were left. Jeremy saw the rest of the colors fly outside of the warehouse. Perhaps going back to their original owners. To its dismay, the creature no longer had any memories to feed off of. Doing what it needed to, to survive, in a swift movement, the tentacle reached for the nearest person to the rift: Mr. Mortimer. It soon wrapped itself like a spiral around the vendor, and trapped him in its grip. Its suction cupped mouths closed in on every opening of skin it could find. Mortimer, mortified, was unable to release its tightening grip on him, as it sucked and sucked, what looked to be one, a few, and every last memory the vendor had amassed in his sixty something existence. And only when it was satisfied did it drop Mortimer to the ground, leaving nothing but a catatonic vegetable who drooled and wet himself.

Still stunned at what both he and Kate saw, Jeremy spoke. "I don't think it'll just stop with him, Kate. It's hungry, and it wants more!"

"I know, but my gun is too close to it!"

"Then we better make this one count." With all his might, Jeremy threw the pistol towards the third machine, which struck it hard, and caused it to dent and fall over. The active mechanisms that kept the opening present were now upset. The machine caused the rift to become unstable, and the creature, which sensed this, pulled back. But it was already too late. The rift collapsed and caused the tenticle to get sliced from the fabric of reality from the other dimension. What was left in this dimension dropped from mid-air with a loud wet slap on what little of Mr. Mortimer remained.

After a few moments, Jeremy helped Kate sit up. Both knew she needed to have her wound looked after. "It's time to return to normal time, Kate."

Already, she was able to recall what Mr. Mortimer had taken from her. Her face seemed smoother and livelier than ever before, which caused her to look younger, somehow.

"You know, you're pretty cute when you have your entire memory back" he playfully said.

"And you're not such a bad shot when you get an adrenaline rush" she fired back.

Jeremy brought the time stopping machine closer to him, and turned the key. "I think we should do this together." He then took her hand, under his, and lowered the lever of the machine. Both looked back at each other and knew, nothing would ever be the same again.

About The Editor

JULIA T. LYE is a graduate of Carleton University living in Ottawa as she pursues a career in creative writing. Her short stories have been published in the horror anthology, What Lies in Wait, the science fiction anthology, The Stranger Side of Tomorrow, and the romance anthology, You Hit Me With Your Car (and Other Love Stories), and her debut novel, Anelisha Knight in the Yarns of Gods, was published by Deebee Books in May of 2019. When she isn't tapping away at her keyboard, she likes to run original dungeons and dragons campaigns, read any book she can get her hands on, and create digital art. You can reach her at lyejulia@gmail.com or check out her website at www.julialye.com

ACKNOWLEDGMENTS

This collection of short stories would not have been possible without the energy and enthusiasm of the Ottawa Workshop writers who contributed their talents to it. These stories emerged from the Fall 2019 Science Fiction and Fantasy workshop held in Ottawa.

Thanks for reading! If you enjoyed this collection, please add a short review on Amazon and/or Goodreads.

Reviews mean a lot to writers, so I encourage you to support our growing writers' community by taking a few minutes now to rate this collection and write a few words of encouragement about it. And please share your copy of the book with others!